Richard Herne Shepherd

The Bibliography of Dickens

a bibliographical list, arranged in chronological order, of the published

writings in prose and verse of Charles Dickens - from 1834 to 1880

Richard Herne Shepherd

The Bibliography of Dickens
a bibliographical list, arranged in chronological order, of the published writings in prose and verse of Charles Dickens - from 1834 to 1880

ISBN/EAN: 9783337368517

Printed in Europe, USA, Canada, Australia, Japan

Cover: Foto ©Andreas Hilbeck / pixelio.de

More available books at **www.hansebooks.com**

THE

Bibliography of Dickens,

A BIBLIOGRAPHICAL LIST

ARRANGED IN CHRONOLOGICAL ORDER

OF THE

PUBLISHED WRITINGS IN PROSE AND VERSE

OF

CHARLES DICKENS

(FROM 1834 TO 1880).

PREFACE.

I have spared no pains to make this Bibliography exhaustive as well as accurate. Like its predecessor, THE BIBLIOGRAPHY OF RUSKIN, it is arranged mainly, though not entirely, in chronological order; and includes all the accessible printed utterances of CHARLES DICKENS that have come under my notice; not merely his larger and smaller separate works, but his scattered and uncollected contributions to journals, magazines, annuals, and keepsakes, his Letters to newspapers and to friends, and his Speeches. No entry has been made at second-hand.

I cannot be sure that my enumeration of the uncollected Letters is absolutely complete, and I shall be greatly indebted to any correspondent who will send me supplementary data for that portion of the work. It should be understood that the letters must have been printed somewhere; that it is not within the scheme and scope of the present compilation to include autograph letters, unless deposited in some national Library or Museum.

I trust that the little work will prove useful to collectors and students, most of whom, I anticipate, will find some information in it that is new to them.

RICHARD HERNE SHEPHERD.

5, BRAMERTON-STREET,
    KING'S-ROAD, CHELSEA :
        Easter, 1880.

BIBLIOGRAPHY OF DICKENS.

1

Sketches contributed to *The Monthly Magazine, or British Register of Politics, Literature, Art, Science and the Belles Lettres.* New Series. London: published by Cochrane and Macrone, and afterwards by James Cochrane & Co., Waterloo-place, Pall Mall. Vols. xvii. to xix. 1834—1835.

Vol. xvii.

pp. 11-18. Mrs. Joseph Porter, ' over the way.' —January, 1834.

,, 151-162. Horatio Sparkins. — February, 1834.

,, 375-386. The Bloomsbury Christening. —April, 1834.

B

pp. 481-493. The Boarding House. — May,
1834.

Vol. xviii.

pp. 177-192. The Boarding House, No. II.*—
August, 1834.

„ 288-295. The " Goings on " at Bramsby
Hall.—September, 1834.†

„ 360-376. The Steam Excursion.—October,
1834.

Vol. xix.

pp. 15-24. Passage in the Life of Mr. Watkins
Tottle.   Chapter the First.—January,
1835.

„ 121-137. *Ib.* Chapter the Second.—
February, 1835.

2

SKETCHES OF LONDON, signed " Boz," in *The Evening
Chronicle.* 1835.

No. 1. Hackney - Coach   Stands. — Saturday,
January 31.

---

* This was the first paper to which the author appended the
signature of " Boz." The previous Sketches appeared anonymously.

† This Sketch is signed " W. P."

No. 2. Gin Shops.—Saturday, February 7.

No. 3. Early Coaches.—Thursday, February 19.

No. 4. The Parish.—Saturday, February 28.

No. 5. " The House."—Saturday, March 7.

No. 6. London Recreations.—Tuesday, March 17.

No. 7. Public Dinners.—Tuesday, April 7.

No. 8. Bellamy's.—Saturday, April 11.

No. 9. Greenwich Fair.—Thursday, April 16.

No. 10. Thoughts about People.—Thursday, April 23.

No. 11. Astley's.—Saturday, May 9.

No. 12. Our Parish.—Tuesday, May 19.

No. 13. The River.—Saturday, June 6.

No. 14. Our Parish.—Thursday, June 18.

No. 15. The Pawnbroker's Shop.—Tuesday, June 30.

No. 16. Our Parish.—Tuesday, July 14.

No. 17. The Streets — Morning. — Tuesday, July 21.

No. 18. Our Parish—Mr. Bung's Narrative.— Tuesday, July 28.

No. 19. Private Theatres.—Tuesday, August 11.

No. 20. Our Parish.—Thursday, August 20.

3

SCENES AND CHARACTERS (signed "Tibbs"), printed in *Bell's Life in London and Sporting Chronicle*, 1835-1836.

1835.

No. 1. Seven Dials.—September 27.

No. 2. Miss Evans and "the Eagle."— October 4.

No. 3. The Dancing Academy.—October 11.

No. 4. Making a Night of it.—October 18.

No. 5. Love and Oysters.—October 25.

> Entitled in the collected "Sketches," *Misplaced Attachment of Mr. John Dounce.*

No. 6. Some Account of an Omnibus Cad.— November 1.

> Begins "Mr. William Barker was born," and differs materially in the concluding part from "The Last Cab Driver and the First Omnibus Cad," as re-published in the collected "Sketches."

No. 7. The Vocal Dress-Maker.—November 22.

> Entitled in the collected "Sketches," *The Mistaken Milliner.*

No. 8. The Prisoners' Van.—November 29.

> Two long opening paragraphs omitted in the collected "Sketches."

No. 9. The Parlour.—December 13.

> Entitled *The Parlour Orator* in the collected "Sketches," where the opening paragraph is omitted.

No. 10. Christmas Festivities.—December 27.

> The concluding paragraph is omitted in the collected "Sketches," where the title is changed to *A Christmas Dinner*.

1836.

No. 11. The New Year.—January 3.

No. 12. The Streets at Night.—January 17.

4

The Tuggs's at Ramsgate (with two illustrations by Seymour).—A Little Talk about Spring and the Sweeps (with an illustration).—Printed in the *Library of Fiction, or Family Story-Teller, consisting of original Tales, Essays, and Sketches of Character*. London: Chapman and Hall. Vol. i. (1836), pp. 1-18 ; 113-119 (both signed "Boz").

5

SKETCHES BY "BOZ," ILLUSTRATIVE OF EVERY-DAY LIFE AND EVERY-DAY PEOPLE. In Two Volumes. With sixteen illustrations by George Cruikshank. London : John Macrone, St. James's-square. 1836.

The first volume (pp. viii. 348) contains The Parish, in six chapters ; Miss Evans and "The Eagle ;" Shops and their Tenants ; Thoughts about People ; A Visit to Newgate ; London Recreations ; The Boarding House, in two chapters ; Hackney Coach Stands ; Brokers and Marine Store Shops ; The Blooms- bury Christening ; Gin Shops ; Public Dinners ; Astley's ; Greenwich Fair ; The Prisoners' Van ; A Christmas Dinner.

The second volume (pp. 342) contains Passage in the Life of Mr. Watkins Tottle, in two chapters ; The Black Veil ; Shabby- genteel People ; Horatio Sparkins ; The Pawnbroker's Shop ; The Dancing Academy ; Early Coaches ; The River ; Private Theatres ; The Great Winglebury Duel ; Omnibuses ; Mrs. Joseph Porter ; The Steam Excursion ; Sentiment.

The Preface to these two volumes is dated "Furnival's Inn, February, 1836."

A second edition appeared in the same year, with a new pre- face, dated "Furnival's Inn, 1st August, 1836."

6

SKETCHES BY "BOZ," ILLUSTRATIVE OF EVERY-DAY LIFE AND EVERY-DAY PEOPLE. The Second Series. London : John Macrone. 1836, pp. viii. 375.

Containing The Streets by Morning ; The Streets by Night ; Making a Night of it ; Criminal Courts ; Scotland Yard ; The

New Year; Meditations in Monmouth Street; Our Next Door Neighbours; The Hospital Patient; Seven Dials; The Mistaken Milliner; Doctors' Commons; Misplaced Attachment of Mr. John Dounce; Vauxhall Gardens by Day; A Parliamentary Sketch, with a few Portraits; Mr. Minns and his Cousin; The Last Cab Driver, and the First Omnibus Cad; The Parlour Orator; The First of May; The Drunkard's Death. With twelve illustrations by George Cruikshank.

The Preface to this third volume is dated "Furnival's Inn, December 17, 1836."

First Complete Edition of the Two Series, with forty illustrations by George Cruikshank. In twenty monthly parts, demy 8vo, commencing November, 1837, and ending June, 1839. Twenty-seven of the twenty-eight illustrations to the former editions—(one illustration, "The Free and Easy" in *The Streets : Night,* being cancelled)—were re-drawn and engraved to suit the larger-sized page of this edition. To these were added thirteen new etchings. There was also a design on the first page of the pink wrapper by George Cruikshank. Preface dated "May 15, 1839." London : Chapman and Hall, 186, Strand. 1839, pp. 526.

The First Series of the *Sketches* comprised, as we have seen (including six chapters of "Our Parish"), thirty-five articles. The Second Series comprised twenty articles. The Complete Edition included all the above, with one additional sketch, viz., "The Tuggs's at Ramsgate;" re-arranged under the headings,—*Sketches from our Parish,* 7; *Scenes,* 25; *Characters,* 12; and *Tales,* 12.

A new Preface, dated "London, October, 1850," was prefixed to the first cheap edition.

7

Sunday under Three Heads : as it is ; as Sabbath Bills would make it ; as it might be made. By

Timothy Sparks. Illustrated by H. K. B. London : Chapman and Hall. 1836, pp. v. 49.

"H. K. B." was Hablot K. Browne ("Phiz"), who was chosen to continue the illustrations to the *Pickwick Papers* after Seymour's death.

EARLY DRAMATIC PIECES.

8

THE STRANGE GENTLEMAN : A Comic Burletta in Two Acts. By "Boz." With etched frontispiece by "Phiz." Performed at the St. James's Theatre, September 29, 1836. London : Chapman and Hall. 1837, pp. 64, in wrapper.

Founded on one of the *Sketches by Boz*, entitled "The Great Winglebury Duel."

9

THE VILLAGE COQUETTES: A Comic Opera. In Two Acts. By Charles Dickens. The Music by John Hullah. London : Richard Bentley. 1836, pp. 71.

The Dedication to J. P. Harley is dated December 15, 1836.

10

Is SHE HIS WIFE ? or, Something Singular : A Comic Burletta, in One Act. By Charles Dickens. Boston : James R. Osgood & Co. 1877, pp. 80.

First performed at the St. James's Theatre, Monday, March 6, 1837.

11

THE LAMPLIGHTER : A Farce. By Charles Dickens (1838). Now first printed from a manuscript in the Forster Collection at the South Kensington Museum. London : 1879, pp. 45, in wrapper.

Only 250 copies privately printed. This farce was withdrawn and never acted.

"He wrote a farce by way of helping the Covent Garden manager, which the actors could not agree about, and which he turned afterwards into a story called *The Lamplighter*. He read the piece at the theatre before the same stage manager to whom he had written to request a very different audience in the same green-room a few years before ; and Dickens could not but fancy that into Mr. Bartley's face, as he listened to the humorous reading, there crept some strange bewildered half-consciousness that in the famous writer he saw again the youthful would-be actor."—FORSTER'S *Life of Dickens*, vol. i, pp. 12 -1.

12.

THE POSTHUMOUS PAPERS OF THE PICKWICK CLUB. Being a faithful Record of the Perambulations, Perils, Travels, Adventures, and Sporting Transactions of the Corresponding Members. Edited by "Boz." With forty-three illustrations by R. Seymour, Buss, and "Phiz" (Hablot K. Browne). In twenty monthly parts, commencing April, 1836, and ending November, 1837 (Parts 19 and 20 forming a double number).* London : Chapman and Hall, 186, Strand. 1837, pp. xvi. 609.

The Dedication to Serjeant Talfourd is dated "48, Doughty-street, September 27, 1837."

The first two numbers contained each only 24 pages of letter-press, the first contained four and the second three illustrations by Seymour, who died suddenly April 20, 1836, while the second number was in preparation. The third and succeeding numbers contained each 32 pages of letterpress, with only two illustrations. Those in the third number were originally executed by a Mr. Buss, but his plates were replaced in later issues of the number by two different designs executed by Mr. Hablot Browne ("Phiz"), who illustrated the remainder of this and many subsequent works of Charles Dickens. The original green wrapper had a design by Seymour, representing scenes of fishing and shooting, and groups of sporting implements. Part ii. contained a notice respecting Seymour's death. Part x. an "Address" from the author to his readers, dated "December, 1836," and Part xv. another "Address," dated "186, Strand, June 30, 1837."

The first cheap Edition contains a new Preface, dated "London, September, 1847." This Preface was considerably amplified in the "Charles Dickens" edition (Chapman and Hall, 1867, pp. xii. 497).

* No number was issued for June, 1837. The fourteenth number bears date "May, 1837" and the fifteenth "July, 1837 :" the publication was suspended during that interval through a severe shock which the author received from the death of a younger sister of his wife (Mary Hogarth).

13

OLIVER TWIST ; OR, THE PARISH BOY'S PROGRESS.
Commenced in the second number of *Bentley's
Miscellany*, in February, 1837, and concluded
in March, 1839. Published in three volumes,
post 8vo, in advance of its completion in the
Miscellany, in October, 1838, with twenty-four
illustrations by George Cruikshank.* London :
Richard Bentley, New Burlington-street. 1838.

A *Third Edition* was issued with "the Author's Preface to
the Third Edition," dated "Devonshire Terrace, April, 1841."
3 vols. 8vo. London : Chapman and Hall. 1841.

---

* The last of these illustrations—*Rose Maylie and Oliver*—as
it appeared in the early copies, was objected to by the author,
and was designed afresh at his request. "The publication had
been announced for October," says Mr. Forster, "but the third-
volume illustrations intercepted it a little. This part of the
story had been written in anticipation of the magazine ; and the
designs for it, having to be executed *in a lump*, were necessarily
done somewhat hastily. The matter supplied in advance of the
monthly portions in the magazine formed the bulk of the last
volume ; and for this the plates had to be prepared by Cruikshank,
also in advance of the magazine, to furnish them in time for the
separate publication. None of these Dickens had seen until he
saw them in the book on the eve of its publication, when he so
strongly objected to one of them that it had to be cancelled.
' I returned suddenly to town yesterday afternoon,' he wrote to
the artist at the end of October, ' to look at the latter pages of
Oliver Twist before it was delivered to the booksellers, when I saw
the majority of the plates in the last volume for the first time.
With reference to the last one—*Rose Maylie and Oliver*—I am
quite sure there can be little difference of opinion between us with
respect to the result. May I ask you whether you will object to
designing this plate afresh, and doing so *at once*, in order that as
few impressions as possible of the present one may go forth ? ' "
FORSTER'S *Life of Dickens.*

Edition in One Volume. Issued with the same plates as the former editions, in ten monthly parts, demy 8vo, uniform with *Pickwick*, commencing January, 1846. The first page of the green wrapper was from a design by George Cruikshank, and depicted eleven scenes (mostly different from those represented in the body of the work), illustrating incidents in the novel, pp. 311. London: published for the Author by Bradbury and Evans, Whitefriars, 1846.

The first cheap Edition contains a new Preface, dated "Devonshire Terrace, March, 1850." This Preface was considerably modified and abridged in the "Charles Dickens" edition (Chapman and Hall, 1867, pp. viii. 258), and a new paragraph was added at the end.

14

Contributions to *Bentley's Miscellany*, 1837-1839. London: Richard Bentley, New Burlington-street.

Vol i.

pp. 49-63. Public Life of Mr. Tulrumble, once Mayor of Mudfog. (Signed "Boz.") With an illustration by George Cruikshank. January, 1837.

„ 291-297. Stray Chapters by "Boz." Chapter 1. The Pantomime of Life. March, 1837.

pp. 515-518. Stray Chapters by "Boz." Chapter 2. Some particulars concerning a Lion. May, 1837.

Editor's Address on the Completion of the First Volume, signed " Boz," and dated "London, June, 1837."

Vol. ii.

pp. 397-413. Full Report of the First Meeting of the Mudfog Association for the Advancement of Everything. Signed "Boz." October, 1837.

Address, signed " Boz," and dated " 30th November, 1837."

Vol. iv.

pp. 209-227. Full Report of the Second Meeting of the Mudfog Association for the Advancement of Everything. With an illustration by George Cruikshank. September, 1838.

Vol. v.

pp. 219-220. Familiar Epistle from a Parent to a Child aged two years and two months, signed " Boz." February, 1839

15

SKETCHES OF YOUNG GENTLEMEN. Dedicated to the Young Ladies. With six Illustrations by "Phiz" [H. K. Browne], small 8vo. London: Chapman and Hall. 1838, pp. viii. 76.

16

SKETCHES OF YOUNG COUPLES; with an urgent Remonstrance to the Gentlemen of England (being Bachelors or Widowers), on the present alarming crisis. By the Author of "Sketches of Young Gentlemen." With six Illustrations by "Phiz" [H. K. Browne]. London: Chapman and Hall. 1840, pp. 92 (including title and half-title).

17

THE LIFE AND ADVENTURES OF NICHOLAS NICKLEBY. With 39 illustrations by Phiz; and Portrait of the Author after Maclise, engraved by Finden. In twenty monthly parts, demy 8vo, commencing April, 1838, and ending October, 1839,—parts 19 and 20 forming a double number, pp. xvi. 624. Inscribed to W. C. Macready. London: Chapman and Hall, 186, Strand. 1839.

Nicholas Nicklcby was heralded by a mock "Proclamation" of three pages demy 8vo, signed "Boz," and dated "February 28, 1838," which will be found stitched in old reviews and magazines of that date.

The first cheap Edition contains a new Preface, dated "Devonshire Terrace, May, 1848."

18

MEMOIRS OF JOSEPH GRIMALDI. Edited by "Boz." With twelve illustrations by George Cruikshank. In two volumes, post 8vo, pp. xix. 288; pp. ix. 268. London : Richard Bentley, 1838.

The Preface is dated "Doughty-street, February, 1838." This Memoir was only edited by Charles Dickens, not written by him.

19

Notice of Mr. John Gibson Lockhart's pamphlet "The Ballantyne Humbug handled." Printed in *The Examiner* of March 31, 1839.

Allusion is made in this notice to a previous one of Ballantyne's *Refutation*. There is a notice of the "Reply to Mr. Lockhart's pamphlet" in *The Examiner* of September 29, 1839.

Written and printed in the *Examiner*, "to express publicly," says Mr. Forster, "his hearty sympathy with Lockhart's handling of some passages in his admirable Life of Scott that had drawn down upon him the wrath of the Ballantynes."

20

Notice of Hood's "Up the Rhine." Printed in *The Examiner*.

"I find him noticing, in the *Examiner*, a book by Thomas Hood ('Up the Rhine'): 'rather poor, but I have not said so, because Hood is too, and ill besides.'"—FORSTER'S *Life of Dickens* (ed. 1876, vol. i., p. 121).

21

MASTER HUMPHREY'S CLOCK. With illustrations on wood by George Cattermole and H. K. Browne; George Cruikshank and Daniel Maclise. In eighty-eight weekly numbers, imperial 8vo, commencing April 4, 1840, and ending November 27, 1841, and in twenty monthly parts,—forming three volumes. Vol. i., pp. iv. 306; vol. ii., pp. vi. 306; vol. iii., pp. vi. 426. London: Chapman and Hall, 186, Strand. 1840-41.

The Old Curiosity Shop began at page 37 of the first volume, and continued, with occasional interruptions in its early part from the intercalary Pickwickian and other chapters, to page 223 of the second volume.

[The first cheap Edition of *The Old Curiosity Shop* contained a new Preface, dated "London, September, 1848."]

Barnaby Rudge began at page 229 of the second volume, and was finished with its 82nd chapter at page 420 of the third volume, after which the *Clock* was wound up by a closing chapter from Master Humphrey (pp. 421-426).

[The first cheap Edition of *Barnaby Rudge* contained a new Preface, dated " London, March, 1849."]

The first volume of *Master Humphrey's Clock* was dedicated to Samuel Rogers, and the Preface was dated " Devonshire Terrace, September, 1840." The Preface of the second volume was dated " Devonshire Terrace, March, 1841;" and the Preface of the third and concluding volume, "Devonshire Terrace, November, 1841."

22

THE FINE OLD ENGLISH GENTLEMAN. New version (to be said or sung at all Conservative dinners). A squib in verse, of eight stanzas, forty-eight lines. Printed in *The Examiner*, Saturday, August 7, 1841, p. 500.

Seven of the eight stanzas of this squib are quoted by Mr. Forster in the twelfth chapter of Book ii. of his *Life of Dickens*. Mr. Forster professes to give it entire, and states that it " had no touch of personal satire in it," and that Dickens " would himself, for that reason, have least objected to its revival." The stanza omitted by Mr. Forster is the sixth, which runs thus :—

" Those were the days for taxes, and for war's infernal din ;
For scarcity of bread, that fine old dowagers might win ;
For shutting men of letters up, through iron bars to grin,
Because they didn't think the Prince was altogether thin,
       In the fine old English Tory times ;
       Soon may they come again !"

23

THE QUACK DOCTOR'S PROCLAMATION. (Tune : " A Cobbler there was.") A squib in verse, of nine

c

stanzas, thirty-six lines. Printed in *The Examiner*,
Saturday, August 14, 1841, p. 517.

Three stanzas of this squib are quoted by Mr. Forster in his
Life of Dickens, Book ii., § 12.

24

SUBJECTS FOR PAINTERS. After Peter Pindar. A
squib in rhyme, seventy lines. Printed in *The
Examiner*, Saturday, August 21, 1841, p. 532.

A few stanzas of this squib are quoted by Mr. Forster in his
Life of Dickens, Book ii., § xii.

"He sent me some rhymed squibs as his anonymous contri-
bution to the fight the Liberals were then making against what
was believed to be intended by the return to office of the Tories.
I doubt if he ever enjoyed anything more than the power of thus
taking part occasionally, unknown to outsiders, in the sharp con-
flict the press was waging at the time."— FORSTER'S *Life of
Dickens*, ed. 1876, vol. i., pp. 186-187.

25

THE LAMPLIGHTER'S STORY.—Printed in *The Pic Nic
Papers by various hands, edited by Charles Dickens,
Esq.* London: Henry Colburn. 1841. Vol. i.,
pp. 1-32.

26

Circular Letter on International Copyright with
America, dated "Devonshire Terrace, July 7,
1842," and signed "Charles Dickens."

This letter, in printed form, was sent to all the principal English authors then living. It was reprinted *in extenso* in the *Morning Chronicle* of Thursday, July 14, in the *Athenæum* and *Examiner* of July 16, 1842, and doubtless in other leading journals.

27

Prologue to Mr. Westland Marston's Play, "The Patrician's Daughter." Written by Mr. Charles Dickens, and spoken by Mr. Macready. (48 lines.) Printed in *The Theatrical Journal and Stranger's Guide*, No. 157, Saturday, December 17, 1842 (Vol. iii., p. 407).

This Prologue was not printed *in extenso* in any of the newspapers, nor with the play itself, which indeed had been published in the previous year (1841), before it was produced on the stage. It appears, with some variations from the above version, in the first volume of the recently-published collection of Charles Dickens's Letters (pp. 77-78).

28

AMERICAN NOTES for General Circulation. By Charles Dickens. In Two Volumes, post 8vo, pp. xvi. 308; vii. 306. London: Chapman and Hall, 186, Strand. 1842.

The first cheap Edition contained a new Preface, dated "London, June 22, 1850."

29

To the Editor of the *Times*.—Letter dated " Devon-shire Terrace, Sunday, Jan. 15," and signed " Charles Dickens."—Printed in *The Times*, Mon-day, January 16, 1843.

In contradiction of a statement made in a notice of *American Notes* (by Mr. James Spedding), published in the *Edinburgh Review* of January, 1843.

30

THE LIFE AND ADVENTURES OF MARTIN CHUZZLEWIT—his Relations, Friends, and Enemies. Comprising all his wills and his ways: with an Historical Record of what he did and what he didn't ; showing, moreover, who inherited the family plate, who came in for the silver spoons, and who for the wooden ladles : the whole forming a com-plete Key to the House of Chuzzlewit. Edited by Boz. With 40 illustrations by H. K. Browne. In twenty monthly parts, demy 8vo, commencing January, 1843, and ending July, 1844,—parts 19 and 20 forming a double number. One volume, pp. xiv. 624. Dedicated to Miss Burdett Coutts.

Preface dated "London, June 25, 1844." London : Chapman and Hall. 1844.

The first cheap Edition contained a new Preface, dated "London, November, 1849."

31

A CHRISTMAS CAROL IN PROSE. Being a Ghost Story of Christmas. By Charles Dickens. With illustrations by John Leech, fcp. 8vo, pp. 166. London : Chapman and Hall, 1843.

The title-page is in red and blue, and the full-page illustrations are coloured. The Preface is dated "December, 1843."

32

A WORD IN SEASON. By Charles Dickens. 32 lines of verse in 4 stanzas. Printed in *The Keepsake* for 1844, edited by the Countess of Blessington. 8vo. London : Longmans, pp. 73, 74.

33

Letter to the Committee of the Metropolitan Drapers' Association, dated "Devonshire Terrace, 28th March, 1844," and signed "Charles Dickens." Printed in *The Student and Young Men's Advocate, a Magazine of Literature, Science, and Art*, No. 1

(New Series). London : Aylott & Jones, Paternoster-row, January, 1845, p. 19.

34

Threatening Letter to Thomas Hood, from an An-
cient Gentleman. By favour of Charles Dickens.
Printed in *Hood's Magazine and Comic Miscellany*.
May, 1844 (Vol. i., pp. 409-414).

35

Evenings of a Working Man, being the occupation
of his scanty leisure. By John Overs. With a
Preface relative to the Author, by Charles Dickens.
London : T. C. Newby. 1844.

The Preface occupies eight pages and a half, and is dated
"London, June, 1844."

36

!' THE CHIMES : a Goblin Story of some Bells that
rang an Old Year out and a New Year in. By
Charles Dickens. Illustrated by Maclise, Doyle,
Leech, and Clarkson Stanfield. London : Chapman and Hall, 1845, pp. 175.

Published Christmas, 1844.

37

"THE CRICKET ON THE HEARTH. A Fairy Tale of Home. By Charles Dickens. Illustrated by Maclise, Doyle, Clarkson Stanfield, Leech, and Landseer. London: printed and published for the Author by Bradbury and Evans, 1846, pp. 174.

Published December, 1845. Inscribed to Lord Jeffrey.

38

Crime and Education. To the Editors of *The Daily News*. Letter of a column and a half, dated " Wednesday morning, Feb. 4, 1846," and signed " Charles Dickens."—*Daily News*, Wednesday, February 4, 1846.

Descriptive of the writer's visit to a Ragged School.

39

THE HYMN OF THE WILTSHIRE LABOURERS (Five stanzas of eight lines each), signed " Charles Dickens."—Printed in *The Daily News*, Saturday, February 14, 1846.

40

Letters on Social Questions—Capital Punishment. To the Editors of the *Daily News*. Two letters of

two columns each, signed " Charles Dickens."—
Daily News, Monday, March 9, and Friday, March
13, 1846.

41

Ⓒ

PICTURES FROM ITALY. By Charles Dickens. The
Vignette Illustrations on wood, by Samuel Palmer,
pp. 270. London : published for the Author by
Bradbury and Evans. 1846.

The substance of this little volume appeared originally in the
Daily News, 1846, under the title of "Travelling Letters. Written
on the Road. By Charles Dickens." The Letters were seven in
number, and appeared on the following dates :—

No. 1. Wednesday, January 21.
No. 2. Lyons, the Rhone, and the Goblin of Avignon.—
Saturday, January 24.
No. 3. Avignon to Genoa.—Saturday, January 31.
No. 4. A Retreat at Albaro.—Monday, February 9.
No. 5. First Sketch of Genoa. The Streets, Shops, and
Houses.—Monday, February 16.
No. 6. In Genoa.—Thursday, February 26.
No. 7. In Genoa, and out of it.—Monday, March 2.

42

Ⓒ

THE BATTLE OF LIFE. A Love Story. By Charles
Dickens. London: Bradbury and Evans, 1846,
pp. 175. Illustrated by Maclise, Doyle, Leech,
and Clarkson Stanfield.

Published Christmas, 1846.

43

DEALINGS WITH THE FIRM OF DOMBEY AND SON, WHOLESALE, RETAIL, AND FOR EXPORTATION. With forty illustrations by H. K. Browne. In twenty monthly parts, demy 8vo, commencing October, 1846, and ending April, 1848, parts 19 and 20 forming a double number.

Dedicated to the Marchioness of Normanby, with Preface dated " Devonshire Terrace, March 24, 1848." One volume, pp. xvi. 624. London: Bradbury and Evans, 1848.

44

Facts and Figures from Italy. By Don Jeremy Savonarola, Benedictine Monk, addressed during the last two winters to Charles Dickens, Esq., being an Appendix to his "Pictures." London: Richard Bentley, 1847, pp. 809, besides title and separate leaf of "Notice."

NOTICE.

Having engaged the Father who signs himself "D. J. Savonarola," to enter on this correspondence, it only remains for me to say that these *are* his Letters.   CHARLES DICKENS. *Broadstairs, Kent, July* 1, 1847.

The volume concludes with a "Poetical Epistle from Savonarola to Boz," dated Genoa, December 14, 1837. This had already appeared in *Bentley's Miscellany*, January, 1838, with the title of "Poetical Epistle from Father Prout to 'Boz,'" under Dickens's editorship, and enables us to assign the authorship of the whole volume to Father Prout.

45

Notice of " The Drunkard's Children," a Sequel to " The Bottle," in eight plates, by George Cruikshank.—*Examiner*, July 8, 1848, p. 436.

46

Notice of " The Rising Generation," a series of twelve drawings on stone, by John Leech.— *Examiner*, December 30, 1848, p. 838.

47

THE HAUNTED MAN AND THE GHOST'S BARGAIN. A Fancy for Christmas Time. With frontispiece and title engraved on wood after John Tenniel, and fourteen other woodcut illustrations by C. Stanfield, R.A., John Leech, Frank Stone, and John Tenniel, foolscap 8vo, pp. 188. London : Bradbury and Evans. 1848.

Published Christmas, 1848.

The five Christmas books were collected into a single volume in 1852, with a new Preface, dated " London, September, 1852."

48

THE PERSONAL HISTORY, ADVENTURES, EXPERIENCE,
AND OBSERVATION OF DAVID COPPERFIELD, THE
YOUNGER, OF BLUNDERSTONE ROOKERY. Which he
never meant to be published on any account.
With forty illustrations by H. K. Browne. In
twenty monthly parts, demy 8vo, commencing
May, 1849, and ending November, 1850,—parts
19 and 20 forming a double number. Inscribed
to the Hon. Mr. and Mrs. Richard Watson of
Rockingham. Preface dated "London, October,
1850," pp. xvi. 624. London : Bradbury and
Evans. 1850.

In the "Charles Dickens" edition the Preface was considerably altered, and a new paragraph added at the end.

49

To the Editor of the *Times.*—Letter dated "Devonshire-terrace, Tuesday, Nov. 13," and signed
"Charles Dickens."—*Times*, Wednesday, November 14, 1849.

A description of the scene at the execution of the Mannings.

50

A Preliminary Word.—*Household Words*, March 30, 1850 (vol. i., pp. 1-2).

51

The Guild of Literature and Art.—*Household Words*, May 10, 1851 (vol. iii., pp. 145-147).

52

One Man in a Dockyard.—*Household Words*, September 6, 1851 (vol. iii., pp. 553-557).

This was a joint article by Charles Dickens and R. H. Horne, who was a frequent contributor to the early volumes of *Household Words*. Horne wrote the description of the works of the dockyard, and Dickens of the fortifications and country scenery round about. (See "Recollections of Contemporaries," appended to *Letters of Elizabeth Barrett Browning addressed to R. H. Horne*, edited by S. R. Townshend Mayer. London : Bentley, 1877, vol. ii., pp. 271-273.)

53

What Christmas is, as we grow older.—Extra number for Christmas, 1851, of *Household Words, a Weekly Journal, conducted by Charles Dickens*,* pp. 1-3.

* The series of *Household Words* forms nineteen volumes of 620 pages each, apart from Title and Index. The first number is dated Saturday, March 30, 1850, and the 479th and last, Saturday, May 28, 1859. Dickens's contributions to the other Christmas numbers are enumerated further on. The above has never been reprinted.

54

) Mr. Nightingale's Diary: A Farce in One Act. By Charles Dickens. Boston: James R. Osgood and Co., 1877, pp. 96.

First performed at Devonshire House, London, 1851. Partly written by Mark Lemon (see Forster, ii., 84, 1876 ed., where it is called "a joint piece of authorship"). There exists, we believe, a privately-printed English edition, issued at the time of its first performance, but not easily accessible.

55

To be Read at Dusk. By Charles Dickens. Printed in *The Keepsake*, edited by Miss Power, for 1852. London: David Bogue. 8vo, pp. 117-131.

A short story in prose.

56

A Child's History of England. By Charles Dickens.

Vol. I. England from the ancient times to the death of King John. 1852, pp. xi. 210.

Vol. II. England from the reign of Henry III. to the reign of Richard III. 1853, pp. viii. 214.

Vol. III. England from the reign of Henry VII. to the Revolution of 1688. 1854, pp. viii. 321.

Three volumes, small square 8vo.   London :
Bradbury and Evans, 1852-1854.   Each volume
contains a frontispiece by F. W. Topham.

Divided here into thirty-seven chapters, but originally into
forty-five, which first appeared at irregular intervals in *Household
Words*. The first chapter appeared in the number for January
25, 1851 (vol. ii., p. 409), and the last in the number for December
10, 1853 (vol. viii. p. 360).

57

BLEAK HOUSE.   With forty illustrations by H. K.
Browne.   In twenty monthly parts, demy 8vo,
commencing March, 1852, and ending September,
1853,—parts 19 and 20 forming a double number.
Preface dated, "London, August, 1853," pp. xvi.
624.   London: Bradbury and Evans.   1853.

58

Trading in Death.—On the State Funeral of the
Duke of Wellington.—*Household Words*, November
27, 1852 (vol. vi., pp. 241-245).

59

Frauds on the Fairies.—*Household Words*, October 1,
1853 (vol. viii., pp. 97-100).

60

HARD TIMES. For these Times. By Charles
Dickens. London : Bradbury and Evans, 1854,
pp. viii. 352. [Divided into Three Books.]

Inscribed to Thomas Carlyle.

Originally published in weekly instalments in *Household
Words* (vol. ix.), commencing April 1, and concluding August
12, 1854.

61

The late Mr. Justice Talfourd.—*Household Words*,
March 25, 1854 (vol. ix., pp. 117-118).

62

By Rail to Parnassus.—*Household Words*, June 16,
1855 (vol. xi., pp. 477-480).

A delightful notice of Leigh Hunt's *Stories in Verse*. The
writer is supposed to be a poor clerk out of employment, travelling from Waterloo-road to Southampton to present himself to
the firm of Heavahoy Brothers, who buys the volume at the rail-
way-stall and reads it on the journey.

"During Leigh Hunt's life, and after the publication of *Bleak
House*, Charles Dickens wrote a most genial paper about him in
Household Words."—Edmund Ollier in the *Daily News*, Saturday,
June 11, 1870.

63

LITTLE DORRIT. With 40 illustrations by H. K.
Browne. In 20 monthly parts, commencing

December, 1855, and ending June, 1857,—parts
19 and 20 forming a double number. Dedicated
to Clarkson Stanfield. Preface dated "London,
May, 1857," pp. xiv. 625. London : Bradbury
and Evans. 1857.

64

A Nightly Scene in London. *Household Words*,
January 26, 1856 (vol. xiii., pp. 25-27).

65

HYMN of five stanzas (20 lines), commencing " Hear
my prayer, O heavenly Father," printed in " The
Wreck of the Golden Mary," the extra Christmas
number of *Household Words* for Christmas, 1856,
p. 21.

Mr. Forster (*Life of Dickens*, ed. 1876, vol. ii., p. 468) refers
to and quotes a letter from Charles Dickens to the Rev. R. H.
Davies, of Chelsea, respecting this hymn. " The letter referred
to," writes Mr. Davies to the present editor, " was in reply to one
from me to C. D. thanking him on religious grounds for the publication of the hymn. He told me he was much obliged for my
letter, and was the more gratified because he wrote the hymn
himself. I gave the letter to a friend. He sent it to Forster. I
wish I had not given it away. Had I sent it to Forster he would
have made it of more interest, as I should have told him how it
came to be written. My friend is dead, and I do not know what
is become of the letter."

66

VIE ET AVENTURES DE NICOLAS NICKLEBY. Traduit avec l'autorisation de l'Auteur par P. Lorain. Paris : Hachette, 1857.

Contains an Address of the English author to the French public, extending to two pages, and dated "Tavistock House, January 17, 1857."

67

Curious Misprint in the Edinburgh Review.—*Household Words*, August 1, 1857 (vol. xvi., pp. 97-100).

A retort upon the notice of *Little Dorrit* published in the *Edinburgh Review* of July, 1857, under the title of *The License of Modern Novelists*. It relates to the Circumlocution Office and Sir Rowland Hill, and to the fall of houses in Tottenham-court-road, which the reviewer had declared to have suggested the catastrophe in *Little Dorrit*.

68

THE LAZY TOUR OF TWO IDLE APPRENTICES. Printed in *Household Words*, October, 1857 (vol. xvi., pp. 313, 337, 361, 385, 409).

" To the first of these papers Dickens contributed all up to the top of the second column of page 316; to the second, all up to the white line in the second column of page 340; to the third, all except the reflections of Mr. Idle (363-5) ; and the whole of the fourth part. All the rest was by Mr. Wilkie Collins."—FORSTER.

D

69

The Case of the Reformers of the Literary Fund : stated by Charles W. Dilke, Charles Dickens, and John Forster. London : 1858, pp. 16.

70

PERSONAL.—*Household Words*, June 12, 1858 (vol. xvii., p. 601).

This is the famous statement respecting his separation from his wife.

71

" REPRINTED PIECES."—Under this title thirty-one sketches that first appeared in *Household Words* from 1850 to 1856 were for the first time collected and acknowledged in the Eighth Volume of the Library Edition of the Works of Charles Dickens, at the end of *The Old Curiosity Shop*. London : Chapman & Hall. 1858, pp. 153-435.

The " Reprinted Pieces" originally appeared in *Household Words* in the following order :—

1850.

A Child's Dream of a Star.—April 6.

The Begging Letter-Writer.—May 18.

A Walk in a Workhouse.—May 25.

The Ghost of Art.—July 20.

The Detective Police.—July 27, August 10.

Three Detective Anecdotes.—September 14.

A Poor Man's Tale of a Patent.—October 19.

A Christmas Tree.—December 21.

1851.

"Births—Mrs. Meek of a Son."—February 22.

A Monument of French Folly.—March 8.

Bill Sticking.—March 22.

On Duty with Inspector Field.—June 14.

Our English Watering Place.—August 2.

A Flight.—August 30.

Our School.—October 11.

1852.

A Plated Article.—April 24.

Our Honourable Friend.—July 31.

Our Vestry.—August 28.

Our Bore.—October 9.

Lying Awake.—October 30.

The Poor Relation's Story.
The Child's Story.—December 25. (Christmas
    Number.)

1853.

Down with the Tide.—February 5.

The Noble Savage.—June 11.

{ The Schoolboy's Story.

Nobody's Story. — December 26. (Christmas Number.)

The Long Voyage.—December 31.

1854.

Our French Watering Place.—November 4.

1855.

Prince Bull : a fairy tale.—February 17.

Out of Town.—September 29.

1856.

Out of the Season.—June 28.

Among these are Dickens's contributions to the Christmas numbers of 1850, 1852, and 1853.

72

A Last Household Word. — Printed in *Household Words*, No. 479, Saturday, May 28, 1859 (vol. xix., p. 620).

73

The Poor Man and his Beer.—*All the Year Round*, April 30, 1859* (vol. i., pp. 13-16).

* The first number of "*All the Year Round*, a Weekly Journal conducted by Charles Dickens," bears date Saturday, April 30, 1859.

74

The Blacksmith. A Trade Song.—*All the Year Round*,
April 30, 1859 (vol. i., p. 20).

"Composed by Mr. Dickens and repeated to me while he was
walking about."—Letter from Rev. T. B. Lawes, of Rothamsted,
St. Alban's, quoted by Mr. Forster in his Life of Dickens (ed.
1876, vol. ii., p. 285).

75

A TALE OF TWO CITIES. In Three Books. By
Charles Dickens.

Published in weekly instalments in *All the Year Round*, commencing in the first number, April 30, 1859 (vol. i., p. 1), and
ending in the thirty-first, November 26, 1859 (vol. ii., p. 95). Also
published in monthly parts, with illustrations by Hablot K.
Browne, the first part bearing date June and the last December,
1859, parts 7 and 8 forming a double number. Inscribed to
Lord John Russell. Preface dated "Tavistock House, November, 1859." London : Chapman & Hall, 193, Piccadilly, 1859,
pp. ix. 254.

76

HUNTED DOWN. A Story in Two Portions.—Printed
in *The New York Ledger* of August 20 and 27 and
September 3, 1859, illustrated with seven wood-
cuts. Reprinted in *All the Year Round*, August
4 and 11, 1860 (vol. iii., pp. 397-400; 422-427).

77

Leigh Hunt. A Remonstrance.—*A.Y.R.*, December 24, 1859 (vol. ii., pp. 206-208).

In reference to the current statement that Leigh Hunt was the original of Harold Skimpole in *Bleak House.*

78

THE UNCOMMERCIAL TRAVELLER. By Charles Dickens. London : Chapman and Hall. 1861, pp. 264.

Contains seventeen papers reprinted from *All the Year Round.* The Preface is dated December, 1860.

These seventeen papers appeared in *All the Year Round* in 1860 as follows :—

Vol. II.

His General Line of Business.—The Shipwreck [of the Royal Charter].—January 28, pp. 321—326.

Wapping Workhouse.—February 18, pp. 392—396.

Two Views of a Cheap Theatre.—February 25, pp. 416.—421.

Poor Mercantile Jack.—March 10, pp. 462—466.

Refreshments for Travellers.—March 24, pp. 512 - 516.

Travelling Abroad.—April 7, pp. 557—562.

Vol. III.

The Great Tasmania's Cargo.—April 21, pp. 37—40.

City of London Churches.—May 5, pp. 85—89.

Shy Neighbourhoods.—May 26, pp. 155—159.

Tramps.—June 16, pp. 230—234.

Dullborough Town.—June 30, pp. 274—278.

Night Walks.—July 21, pp. 348—352.

Chambers.—August 18, pp. 452—456.

Nurses' Stories.—September 8, pp. 517—521.

Arcadian London.—September 29, pp. 588—591.

Vol. IV.

The Italian Prisoner.—October 13, pp. 13—17.

79

GREAT EXPECTATIONS. By Charles Dickens. In Three Volumes, pp. 344, 351, 344. London: Chapman and Hall. 1861.

Inscribed to Chauncy Hare Townshend.

Originally published in weekly instalments in *All the Year Round*, where it commenced December 1, 1860 (voL iv., p. 169), and ended August 3, 1861 (voL v., p. 437).

80

To the Editor of The Times. Letter dated "Gad's-hill, Jan. 8," and signed "Charles Dickens."— Printed in *The Times*, Saturday, January 12, 1861.

Refers to a dramatized version of his Christmas story, "A Message from the Sea," announced for performance without his sanction at the Britannia Theatre.

81

Four Stories.—*All the Year Round*, September 14, 1861 (vol. v., pp. 589-593).

82

The Election for Finsbury.—To the Editor of the *Daily News*. Letter dated "Newcastle-on-Tyne, Nov. 21," and signed "Charles Dickens."—*Daily News*, Saturday, November 23, 1861.

83

The Earthquake. To the Editor of the *Times.*—Letter dated " Gad's-hill-place, Higham by Rochester, Oct. 7," and signed " Charles Dickens."—*Times,* Thursday, October 8, 1863.

84

Pincher Astray.—*All the Year Round,* January 30, 1864 (vol. x., pp. 539-541).

85

In Memoriam. By Charles Dickens. — *Cornhill Magazine,* February, 1864 (vol. ix., pp. 129-132).

A memorial notice of William Makepeace Thackeray.

86

Our Mutual Friend. With 40 illustrations by Marcus Stone. In 20 monthly parts, commencing May, 1864, and ending November, 1865,—parts 19 and 20 forming a double number. Inscribed to Sir James Emerson Tennent. In two volumes. Vol. i., pp. xi. 320. Vol. ii., pp. viii. 309. "Postscript in lieu of Preface" dated " September 2nd, 1865." London: Chapman and Hall, 193, Piccadilly. 1865.

87

Legends and Lyrics. By Adelaide Anne Procter. With an Introduction by Charles Dickens. London : Bell and Daldy, 1866.

The Introduction occupies eleven pages.

88

History of 'Pickwick.' Letter dated "Gad's Hillplace, March 28, 1866," and signed "Charles Dickens." Printed in *The Athenæum*, March 31, 1866 (p. 430); and note dated "April 3, 1866," and signed "Charles Dickens," correcting a verbal mistake in it.—Printed in the *Athenæum*, April 7, 1866, p. 464.

Respecting Seymour and his illustrations of the first two numbers of *The Pickwick Papers*.

89

The late Mr. Stanfield.—*All the Year Round*, June 1, 1867 (vol. xvii., p. 537).

90

Christmas Stories from *Household Words* and *All the Year Round* (1854-1867). First collected in the

"Charles Dickens" Edition (1871) with 8 illustrations, and in the Illustrated Library Edition (1876) with 14 illustrations.

A posthumous collection of Charles Dickens's contributions to the extra Christmas numbers of his two journals. These were as follows :

HOUSEHOLD WORDS.

1854. "THE SEVEN POOR TRAVELLERS."—1. In the old City of Rochester. 2. The Story of Richard Doubledick. 3. The Road.

1855. "THE HOLLY TREE."—1. Myself. 2. The Boots. 3. The Bill.

1856. "THE WRECK OF THE GOLDEN MARY."—The Wreck.

1857. "THE PERILS OF CERTAIN ENGLISH PRISONERS."— 1. The Island of Silver-store. 2. The Rafts on the River.

1858. "A HOUSE TO LET."—Going into Society.

ALL THE YEAR ROUND.

1859. "THE HAUNTED HOUSE."—1. The Mortals in the House. 2. The Ghost in Master B.'s Room (and a page at the close).

1860. "A MESSAGE FROM THE SEA."—"Nearly all the first and the whole of the second and the last chapter, The Village, The Money, and The Restitution : the two intervening chapters, though also with insertions from his hand, not being his."—FORSTER.

1861. "TOM TIDDLER'S GROUND."—1. Picking up Soot and Cinders. 2. Picking up Miss Kimmeens. 3. Picking up the Tinker.

1862. "SOMEBODY'S LUGGAGE."—1. His leaving it till called for. 2. His Boots. 3. His Brown-paper Parcel. 4. His wonderful end. 5. A portion of the chapter, His Umbrella (not reprinted).

91

THE UNCOMMERCIAL TRAVELLER. By Charles Dickens. With illustrations. London : Chapman and Hall. 1868, pp. 172.

Contains eleven new papers from *All the Year Round* out of the thirteen enumerated below, besides those published in the former edition, making in all twenty-eight papers.

SECOND SERIES OF "THE UNCOMMERCIAL TRAVELLER."

All the Year Round.—1863. ✝

4. The Short-Timers. June 20.
5. Bound for the Great Salt Lake.—July 4.
6. The City of the Absent. —July 18.
7. An Old Stage-Coaching House.—August 1.
8. The Boiled Beef of New England. —August 15.
9. Chatham Dockyard.—August 29.
10. In the French-Flemish Country.—September 12.
11. Medicine-Men of Civilisation.— September 26.
12. Titbull's Almshouses.—October 24.

1868.

13. The Ruffian. —October 10.

Nos. 4 and 13 were first included in the Illustrated Library Edition of Dickens's Works (1875), together with six out of seven of the *New Uncommercial Samples (vide § 95 infrà)*, making in all thirty-six papers.

92

GEORGE SILVERMAN'S EXPLANATION, in nine chapters. Printed in the *Atlantic Monthly*, a Magazine of Literature, Science, Art and Politics. Boston: Ticknor and Fields, January, February, and March, 1868 (vol. xxi., pp. 118-123 ; 145-149 ; 277-283). Published also in *All the Year Round*, February 1, 15 and 29, 1868 (vol. xix., pp. 180-183 ; 228-230 ; 276-281).

93

HOLIDAY ROMANCE. In Four Parts. Printed in *Our Young Folks, an Illustrated Magazine for Boys and*

Girls. Boston : Ticknor and Fields, January,
March, April, and May, 1868, vol. iv., pp. 1-7 ;
129-136 ; 193-200 ; 257-263 (with four full-page
illustrations drawn by Sir John Gilbert and initial-
letter illustrations to each part by G. G. White
and S. Eytinge, junior). Published also in *All the*
Year Round, January 25, February 8, March 14,
and April 4, 1868 (vol. xix., pp. 156-159 ; 204-
208 ; 324-327 ; 396-399).

94

A Debt of Honour. Postscript to the latest-published
editions of *American Notes* and *Martin Chuzzlewit*,
dated " May, 1868," and signed "Charles
Dickens."—*All the Year Round*, June 6, 1868
(vol. xix., p. 610).

95

New Uncommercial Samples. By Charles Dickens.
(All the Year Round, New Series.)

Vol. I.

1. Aboard Ship.—December 5, 1868, pp. 12-17.
2. A Small Star in the East.—December 19,
   1868, pp. 61-66.

3. A Little Dinner in an Hour.—January 2, 1869, pp. 108-111.

4. Mr. Barlow.—January 16, 1869, pp. 156-159.

5. On an Amateur Beat.—February 27, 1869, pp. 300-303.

6. *A Fly-leaf in a Life.—May 22, 1869, pp. 589-591.

Vol. II.

7. A Plea for Total Abstinence.—June 5, 1869, pp. 13-15.

96

Landor's Life. A notice of Mr. Forster's Biography of Walter Savage Landor.—*A. Y. R.*, New Series. July 24, 1869 (vol. ii., pp. 181-185).

This was the last paper contributed by Dickens to *All the Year Round*.

97

On Mr. Fechter's Acting.—*Atlantic Monthly*, Boston, August, 1869 (vol. xxiv., pp. 242-244), signed " Charles Dickens."

Written to introduce Mr. Fechter, who was then about to leave England for a professional tour in the United States, to the American play-going public.

* This "Sample" is not included in any of the Collected Editions.

98

Religious Opinions of the late Reverend Chauncy
Hare Townshend. Published as directed in his
Will by his Literary Executor. London : Chap-
man and Hall. 1869, pp. viii. 293.

The "Explanatory Introduction" by Charles Dickens, the
editor of the volume, occupies two pages.

99

The Mystery of Edwin Drood. With 12 illustrations by S. L. Fildes, and a portrait engraved
on steel from a photograph taken in 1868. In six
monthly parts, commencing April, 1870, and ending September, 1870, pp. viii. 190. London :
Chapman and Hall. 1870.

With Prefatory note dated "12th August, 1870," referring
to the unfinished state in which the story was left at the author's
death.

LETTERS.

100

THE LETTERS OF CHARLES DICKENS. *Edited by his Sister-in-law and his eldest Daughter. In Two Volumes.* Vol. i, pp. ix. 463; vol. ii. pp. 464. London : Chapman and Hall, 1880.

Published November 21, 1879. The Preface is signed "Mamie Dickens, Georgina Hogarth," and is dated "London, October, 1879." The Index was compiled by Henry Fielding Dickens.

ADDITIONAL ERRATA IN FIRST VOLUME.

1838. Narrative, page 7, third paragraph, for "Rev. Thomas Barham" read "Rev. R. H. Barham."

Page 299, line 13, for "W. H. H." *read* "W. H. W."

Two letters to Mr. George Cattermole are wrongly placed :—
1840.

The letter dated "Devonshire Terrace, Friday Morning," and printed on pp. 34-35, instead of coming between the two letters of December 21 and 22, 1840, and breaking their obvious sequence and continuity, should precede the former. It belongs presumably to the month of August : it refers at any rate to "the end of September" as yet to come :—"I want to see you about a frontispiece to our first 'Clock' volume, which will come out (I think) at the end of September."

This letter should be immediately followed by the one dated "Devonshire Terrace, Thursday, August 13," printed at page 47-48, and wrongly assigned to the year 1841. It belongs to the year 1840, as is evident, first, from the date, "*Thursday*, August 13," August 13 falling on Thursday in the year 1840, and on *Friday* in the year 1841 (see previous letter printed on page 46, and dated "*Friday, August 6, 1841*") ; and, secondly, from the nature of the contents : "Will you turn your attention to a frontispiece for *our first volume ?* The volume is not published until the end of September." The first volume of *Master Humphrey's Clock*, to which this refers, was published with a Preface dated "September, 1840." *Vide suprà*, p. 17.

1841.

The second paragraph of "Narrative," on page 37, runs as follows : "The letter to Mr. George Cattermole (26th June) refers to a dinner given to Charles Dickens by the people of Edinburgh on his first visit to that city." No letter of this date, or containing any such reference, appears in the book.

1851.

In the "Narrative," under this date, page 241, it is stated : " This year he wrote and published *The Haunted Man*, which he had found himself unable to finish for the previous Christmas. It was the last of the ' Christmas Books.' "

In the "Narrative" of 1847 it is stated (page 170): " He decided to let this Christmas pass without a story and postponed the publication of *The Haunted Man* until the following year."

Again in the "Narrative" of 1848, page 185: " The autumn months were again spent at Broadstairs, where he wrote *The Haunted Man*, which was illustrated by Mr. Frank Stone, Mr. Leech, and others. . . . The letters to Mr. Stone on the subject of his illustrations to *The Haunted Man* are written from Brighton."

The Haunted Man was in fact published Christmas, 1848.

1853.

The undated and unsigned letter to Mr. Wills, printed p. 299 as the first of the letters of 1853, was evidently written late in the month of November, 1852. It refers to the arrangements for the forthcoming Christmas number and to " Mrs. Gaskell's ghost story," which " I have got this morning" but "not yet read." There is a note to Mrs. Gaskell accompanying a proof of this story, and dated "Dec. 1, 1852," printed at page 292.

E

MEMORANDA.

Narrative 1838, page 7, second paragraph.—"The letter which we give in this year to Mr. Justice Talfourd is, unfortunately, the only one we have been able to procure to that friend." Three other letters to Talfourd are printed in Dr. Shelton Mackenzie's Life of Dickens.

Letter to Douglas Jerrold, dated "Devonshire Terrace, May 3, 1843."—Page 88, line 9.—"There were men there who made" runs in the original letter—"There were men there—your City aristocracy—who made," &c. "Dismal features" (last words of the same paragraph) reads "dismal flatness" in the version of the letter printed by Mr. Blanchard Jerrold; but it would require reference to the original autograph to decide which is correct.

LETTERS OF C. D.	B. J. VERSION.
Page 88, last line but one — "when the princess restores"	"where the Princess restores"

There is a final paragraph in the B. J. version, relating to domestic matters, which disappears in the collected Letters.

Letter to Douglas Jerrold, dated "Devonshire Terrace," June 13, 1843.

Page 90, last line, "I should like to deprive." The opening words of this sentence have slipped out. The B. J. version runs:—"If there were a fine day, I should like to deprive," &c.

Page 91, after "public-spirited individual" (line 20) a humorous passage about Talfourd and Macready is omitted, as is a second paragraph of postscript alluding to Maclise.

Letter to Douglas Jerrold, dated "Household Words Office, March 6, 1856."

LETTERS OF C. D.	B. J. VERSION.
Page 428, line 1, "do battle with the Lords."	"do battle with the love of lords."
ib.—"bestow ourselves."	"bestir ourselves."

B. J. dates this letter "Sixth *February,* 1856."

ADDITIONAL ERRATA IN SECOND VOLUME.

1862.

In the letter to Mr. Baylis, p. 179, five lines from bottom, "she had *better* attach her fernery." The reading of the autograph letter is not "better," but "best."

1868.

In the letter to Mr. Edward Bulwer Lytton Dickens, page 403—

Line 1, omit "ever."

Line 4, for "already" read "always."

Line 8, for "and do this" read "and to do it."

Six lines from bottom (last word of paragraph), for "men" read "Man."

Last line but three, first word, for "wearied" read "harassed." (See this letter as correctly printed in Forster's *Life of Dickens*.)

Page 422. Why should "*Earl* Russell," already so entitled in 1865 (see page 235), figure again in 1869, in the margin, as "The Lord John Russell?"

1870.

The letters to Mrs. Dallas and to Mr. S. L. Fildes, both dated "Jan. 16" (pp. 434-435), should precede the letter to Mr. W. H. Wills, dated "Jan. 23" (pp. 433-434).

MEMORANDA.

In a footnote (editorial) to page 350 it is stated that Mr. H. F. Chorley "was the well-known musical critic, and a dear and intimate friend of Charles Dickens and his family. *We have no letters to him*, Mr. Chorley having destroyed all his correspondence before his death." In the *Autobiography, Memoir and Letters of Henry Fothergill Chorley*, edited by H. G. Hewlett (Bentley, 1873), vol. ii., pp. 161-166, 229-236, are printed six letters from Charles Dickens to Chorley dated between the years 1860 and 1867.

Page 407. The "lady who prefers to be anonymous," authoress of the "remarkable story" called *An Experience*, appears to be a

Miss Jolly (see British Museum Catalogue). Her contributions to *Houschold Words* and *All the Year Round* were republished in three volumes in 1875, under the title of *A Wife's Story and other Tales*, with three letters from Charles Dickens, dated in 1855 and 1869, the last referring to this very story, "An Experience."

The letters in the above collection were addressed to the following correspondents, and bear the lates affixed:—

AGATE, Mr. John:—
Nov. 6, 1861.

AINSWORTH, William Harrison:—
1. April 29, 1841.   3. Oct. 13, 1843.
2. Sept. 14, 1842.

ANONYMOUS:—
1. To an anonymous correspondent, on the Society for the Propagation of the Gospel in Foreign Parts. July 9, 1852.
2. June 4, 1857.
3. To an anonymous correspondent (a struggling artist). Jan. 9, 1861.
4. Feb. 5, 1867, on a MS. Novel.
5. Another "Bobadil" Note. Oct. 11 [1848].

ARMSTRONG, The Misses:—
Feb. 10, 1862.*

* Printed and facsimiled in *St. Nicholas: Scribner's Illustrated Magazine for Girls and Boys*, New York, May, 1877 (vol. iv., pp. 438-441).

AUSTIN, Mr. Henry :—

1. 1833 or 1834.	7. Oct. 7, 1851.
2. May 1, 1842.	8. Oct. 25, 1851.
3. May 12, 1842.	9. Sept. 6, 1854.
4. Sept. 25, 1842.	10. June 6, 1857.
5. Sept. 7, 1851.	11. Aug. 15, 1857.
6. Sept. 21, 1851.	12. Sept. 2, 1857.

AUSTIN, Mrs. Henry :—

1. Nov. 3, 1861.	3. July 21, 1868.
2. Oct. 7, 1862.	

BABBAGE, Mr. Charles :—

1. April 27, 1843.	2. Feb. 26, 1848.

BANCROFT, Mrs. (Marie Wilton) :—
May 31, 1870.

BANKS, Mr. G. Linnæus :—
Dec. 26, 1852.

BAYLIS, Mr. Thomas :—
July 2, 1862.*

BENZON, Miss Lily :—
June 18, 1866.

BICKNELL, Mr. Henry :—
Nov. 28, 1850.

BLANCHARD, Laman :—
January 4, 1844.

* The original autograph of this letter is in the British Museum. "EG. 2,264, ff. 24-25."

BOYLE, Miss Mary : –

1. Sept. 16, 1850.
2. Sept. 20, 1850.
3. Oct. 30, 1850.
4. Feb. 21, 1851.
5. Oct. 10, 1851.
6. July 22, 1852.
7. January 16, 1854.
8. Jan. 3, 1855.
9. Jan. 28, 1856.
10. Feb. 7, 1857.
11. Sept. 10, 1858.
12. Dec. 28, 1860.
13. Nov. 17, 1861.
14. Dec. 28, 1861.
15. Dec. 27, 1862.
16. Jan. 6, 1866.
17. Dec. 4, 1867.
18. Jan. 6, 1869.

BROOKFIELD, Rev. W. H. : —

1. May 17, 1863.
2. May 24, 1863.

BROOKFIELD, Mrs. :—

Feb. 20, 1866.

BROOKS, Shirley :—

1. July 12, 1869.
2. April 1, 1870.

CARLISLE, Lord (Lord Morpeth) :—

1. Aug. 3, 1843.
2. Nov. 28, 1845.
3. July 8, 1851.
4. Aug. 5, 1852.
5. April 15, 1857.
6. Aug. 8, 1860.
7. Nov. 15, 1861.

CARTWRIGHT, Mr. Samuel :—

Jan. 29, 1868.

CATTERMOLE, George :—

1. 1839 (undated).
2. January 13, 1840.
3. 1840 (undated).
4. March 9, 1840.
5. Dec. 21, 1840.
*6. 1840 (undated) Friday morning.
7. Dec. 22, 1840.
8. Jan. 14, 1841.
9. Jan. 28, 1841.
10. Jan. 30, 1841.
11. Feb. 9, 1841.
12. Feb. 26, 1841.
13. July 28, 1841.

* This letter should have been placed before the previous one. It refers to "the end of September" as yet to come.

14. Aug. 6, 1841.

15. Aug. 13 (1840).*

16. Aug. 19, 1841.

17. Sept. 12, 1841.

18. Sept. 21, 1841.

19. Dec. 20, 1842.

20. Aug. 27, 1845.

CATTERMOLE, Mrs. George :—

1. May 16, 1868.

2. July 22, 1868.

CERJAT, M. de :—

1. Nov. 27, 1846.

2. Dec. 29, 1849.

3. Jan. 16, 1854.

4. Jan. 3, 1855.

5. Jan. 17, 1857.

6. July 7, 1858.

7. Feb. 1, 1859.

8. May 3, 1860.

9. Feb. 1, 1861.

10. March 16, 1862.

11. May 28, 1863.

12. Oct. 25, 1864.

13. Nov. 13, 1865.

14. Jan. 1, 1867.

15. Aug. 26, 1868.

16. Jan. 4, 1869.

CHAPMAN AND HALL, Messrs. :—
1842 (undated).

CLARKE, Mr. John :—
March 24, 1869.

COLLINS, Mr. Wilkie :—

1. Dec. 20, 1852.

2. July 12, 1854.

3. Sept. 26, 1854.

4. May 24, 1855.

5. July 17, 1855.

6. Sept. 30, 1855.

7. Jan. 19, 1856.

8. June 6, 1856.

9. July 13, 1856.

10. Jan. 17, 1858.

11. Sept. 6, 1858.

12. Sept. 16, 1859.

13. Jan. 7, 1860.

14. Oct. 24, 1860.

15. Aug. 28, 1861.

16. Oct. 14, 1862.

17. April 22, 1863.

18. Jan. 24, 1864.

19. Jan. 12, 1868.

20. Dec. 8, 1868.

COMPTON, Mrs. :—
Aug. 2, 1857.

* This letter is wrongly placed : it belongs to 1840.

COOKE, Mr. T. P. :—
July 30, 1857.

COSTELLO, Mr. Dudley :—
1. June 7, 1844.   2. January 26, 1849.

CROKER, Mr. Crofton :—
March 6, 1852.

CUNNINGHAM, Mr. Peter :—
1. June 22, 1848.   3. 1853 (undated).
2. Dec. 26, 1851.   4. June 7, 1854.

DALLAS, Mrs. (Miss Glyn) :—
1. 1863 (undated).   2. Jan. 16, 1870.

DEANE, Dr. F. H. :—
April 4, 1842.

DELANE, Mr. John :—
Sept. 12, 1853.

DEVONSHIRE, Duke of :—
1. June 1, 1856.   3. Dec. 1, 1856.
2. July 5, 1856.

Humble Petition of Charles Dickens, a Distressed Foreigner.
Paris, March 3, 1856.

DICKENS, Mrs. Charles :—
1-2. 1835 (undated).   11. Dec. 21, 1846.
3. Feb. 1, 1838.   12. June 16, 1849.
4. Nov. 1, 1838.   13. Sept. 3, 1851.
5. Feb. 26, 1844.   14. Feb. 12, 1851.
6. Nov. 8, 1844.   15. March 26, 1851.
7. Nov. 23, 1844.   16. Nov. 13, 1851.
8. Nov. 28, 1844.   17. Nov. 14, 1853.
9. Dec. 2, 1844.   18. Oct. 16, 1855.
10. Dec. 19, 1846.   19. May 5, 1856.

DICKENS, Miss [Mamie] :—

1. March 4, 1847.	30. Feb. 17, 1867.
2. May 24, 1847 (and Katie D.)	31. Feb. 21, 1867.
3. Aug. 4, 1847.	32. March 16, 1867.
4. Sept. 8, 1848.	33. March 21, 1867.
5. Feb. 27, 1849.	34. Sept. 30, 1867.
6. Oct. 4, 1856.	35. Nov. 10, 1867.
7. Aug. 7, 1858.	36. Nov. 21, 1867.
8. Aug. 12, 1858.	37. Dec. 1, 1867.
9. Aug. 23, 1858.	38. Dec. 11, 1867.
10. Aug. 28, 1858.	39. Dec. 26, 1867.
11. Sept. 15, 1858.	40. Dec. 30, 1867.
12. Oct. 22, 1858.	41. Jan. 13, 1868.
13. June 11, 1859.	42. Jan. 18, 1868.
14. Sept. 2, 1859.	43. Jan. 23, 1868.
15. Sept. 23, 1860.	44. Jan. 31, 1868.
16. Oct. 10, 1861.	45. Feb. 4, 1868.
17. Nov. 4, 1861.	46. Feb. 11, 1868.
18. Nov. 23, 1861.	47. Feb. 25, 1868.
19. Nov. 27, 1861.	48. March 2, 1868.
20. Nov. 29, 1861.	49. March 16, 1868.
21. Jan. 16, 1863.	50. March 29, 30, 31, 1868.
22. Feb. 1, 1863.	51. April 7, 1868.
23. Nov. 14, 1865.	52. Sept. 26, 1868.
24. April 14, 1866.	53. Oct. 12, 1868.
25. April 18, 1866.	54. Dec. 15, 1868.
26. April 20, 1866.	55. Jan. 27, 1869.
27. Jan. 22, 1867.	56. March 5, 1869.
28. Jan. 24, 1867.	57. April 22, 1869.
29. Feb. 1, 1867.	58. Aug. 3, 1869.

DICKENS, Charles, jun. :—

1. Nov. 30, 1867.	2. Jan. 15, 1868.

DICKENS, Edward Bulwer Lytton :—

September, 1868.*

* This Letter had already been printed in Mr. Forster's *Life of Charles Dickens* (ed. 1876, vol. ii., pp. 467-468).

DICKENS, Henry Fielding :—

1. Feb. 11, 1868.
2. Oct. 15, 1868.
3. Feb. 17, 1870.
4. March 29, 1870.

DICKSON, Mr. David :—
May 10, 1843.

DIEZMAN, Mr. S. A. (his German translator) :—
March 10, 1840.

DILKE, Mr. C. W. :—
March 19, 1857.

EELES, Mr. :—

1. Oct. 22, 1851.
2. Nov. 17, 1851.

ELY, Miss Marion (niece of Lady Talfourd) :—
April 19, 1846.

FECHTER, Mr. Charles :—

1. Nov. 4, 1862.
2. Dec. 6, 1862.
3. Feb. 4, 1863.
4. Sept. 4, 1866.
5. Sept. 16, 1867.
6. Feb. 24, 1868.
7. March 3, 1868.
8. 1868 (Oct. ?)
9. Oct. 7, 1868.

FILDES, Mr. S. L. :—
Jan. 16, 1870.

FINLAY, Mr. F. D. :—

1. Sept. 3, 1867.
2. Oct. 4, 1868.
3. Jan. 1, 1869.

FITZGERALD, Mr. Percy :—

1. July 4, 1863.	6. Nov. 6, 1866.
2. July 27, 1864.	7. July 21, 1867.
3. July 7, 1865.	8. July 28, 1867.
4. Sept. 23, 1865.	*9. March 9, 1870.
5. Feb. 2, 1866.	*10. March 11, 1870.

FORSTER, Mr. John :—

1. Dec. 27, 1846.	7. Aug. 25, 1859.
2. April 22, 1848.	8. May 2, 1860.
3. April 14, 1855.	9. Oct. 4, 1860.
4. May 13, 1857.	10. July 1, 1861.
5. Feb. 3, 1858.	11. March 29, 1864.
6. Oct. 10, 1858.	

FRITH, Mr. W. P., R.A. :—

1. Nov. 15, 1842.	3. April 16, 1870.
2. Nov. 17, 1842.	

GASKELL, Mrs. :—

1. January 31, 1850.	6. May 3, 1853.
2. Dec. 5, 1851.	7. April 21, 1854.
3. Dec. 21, 1851.	8. Aug. 17, 1854.
4. Dec. 1, 1852.	9. January 27, 1855.
5. Dec. 17, 1852.	

* The name of the correspondent to whom these two letters were addressed is, with somewhat superfluous mystery, suppressed in the Collected Letters (vol. ii., pp. 436-437). As, however, they were written to a contributor to *All the Year Round*, about to commence a long serial story in that journal, who had another story in progress in the *Gentleman's Magazine* and another announced in *Once a-Week*,—complaining of haste and want of care, &c.,—it does not need a witch to solve the riddle. The novel of "Will he Escape? by Percy Fitzgerald," was appearing at that time in the *Gentleman's Magazine*, and "The Sword of Damocles, or Memoirs of a Successful Family, by Percy Fitzgerald," was announced during February and March to appear in *Once-a-Week*, and commenced in the number for April 9, 1870. *The Doctor's Mixture* commenced (anonymously) in *All the Year Round*, Saturday, June 4, 1870 (the week before Dickens's death), which it is to be hoped it did not accelerate. It was first announced in the number for April 30, 1870.

HALDIMAND, Mr. :—
Nov., 1846.

HALLECK, Fitz-Greene : —
Feb. 14, 1842.

HARLEY, Mr. J. P. :—
1. 1837 (undated).   2. June 28, 1839.

HARNESS, Rev. William :—
1. January 2, 1841.   3. Aug. 19, 1854.
3. Nov. 8, 1842.

HENDERSON, Mrs. :—
July 4, 1867.

HOGARTH, Miss :—
1. Feb. 4, 1845.   21. Aug. 25, 1858.
2. 1847 (undated).   22. Aug. 29, 1858.
3. Dec. 13, 1847.   23. Sept. 11, 1858.
4. Oct. 25, 1853.   24. Sept. 17, 1858.
5. Oct. 29, 1853.   25. Sept. 26, 1858.
6. Nov. 4, 1853.   26. Nov. 3, 1858.
7. Nov. 13, 1853.   27. Sept. 24, 1860.
8. Nov. 25, 1853.   28. Nov. 1, 1860.
9. July 22, 1854.   29. Jan. 9, 1861.
10. Feb. 16, 1855.   30. Oct. 13, 1861.
11. Feb. 8, 1856.   31. Oct 29, 1861.
12. March 11, 1856.   32. Nov. 1, 1861.
13. March 14, 1856.   33. Nov. 7, 1861.
14. May 5, 1856.   34. Nov. 22, 1861.
15. Sept. 9, 1857.   35. Nov. 25, 1861.
16. Sept. 12, 1857.   36. Dec. 3, 1861.
17. Sept. 15, 1857.   37. Jan. 3, 1862.
18. Aug. 5, 1858.   38. Jan. 8, 1862.
19. Aug. 18, 1858.   39. Jan. 28. 1862.
20. Aug. 20, 1858.   40. Feb. 1, 1863.

41. Oct. 7, 1863.
42. Feb. 9, 1866.
43. April 13, 1866.
44. April 17, 1866.
45. April 19, 1866.
46. April 26, 1866.
47. May 11, 1866.
48. Jan. 21, 1867.
49. Jan. 24, 1867.
50. Feb. 15, 1867.
51. Feb. 19, 1867.
52. March 6, 1867.
53. March 15, 1867.
54. March 17, 1867.
55. March 20, 1867.
56. March 29, 1867.
57. Aug. 2,'1867.
58. Sept. 30, 1867.
59. Nov. 13, 1867.
60. Nov. 16-17, 1867.
61. Nov. 25, 1867.
62. Dec. 4, 1867.
63. Dec. 16, 1867.
64. Dec. 22, 1867.
65. Jan. 3, 1868.
66. Jan. 4, 1868.

67. Jan. 12, 1868.
68. Jan. 21, 1868.
69. Jan. 29-30, 1868.
70. Feb. 7, 1868.
71. Feb. 13, 1868.
72. Feb. 17, 1868.
73. Feb. 27-28, 1868.
74. March 8-9, 1868.
75. March 12, 1868.
76. April 1 to 3, 1868.
77. Oct. 11, 1868.
78. Oct. 13, 1868.
79. Dec. 6, 1868.
80. Dec. 12, 1868.
81. Dec. 14, 1868.
82. Dec. 16, 1868.
83. Dec. 18, 1868.
84. Jan. 29, 1869.
85. Feb. 25, 1869.
86. Feb. 26, 1869.
87. March 7, 1869.
88. March 20, 1869.
89. March 21, 1869.
90. April 4, 1869.
91. April 21, 1869.

HOGGE, Mrs. (niece of the Rev. W. Harness) :—
April 14, 1858.

HOOD, Thomas :—
Nov. 30, 1842.

HORNE, Mr. R. H. :—
Nov. 13, 1843.

HORNE, Mrs. :—
Oct. 20, 1856.

HUGHES, Master Hastings :—
Dec. 12, 1838.

HULKES, Mrs. :—
June 18, 1865.

*JERROLD, Douglas :—
1. May 3, 1843.   4. May 26, 1846.
2. June 13, 1843.   5. March 6, 1856.
3. Oct. 16, 1844.

JEWISH LADY :—
1. July 10, 1863.   3. March 1, 1867.
2. Nov. 16, 1864.

JOLL, Miss :—
Nov. 27, 1849.

JONES, Mr. Walter (Committee of the Newsvendors) :
June 17, 1865.

KEELEY, Mr. Robert :—
June 24, 1844.

KENT, Mr. Charles :—
1. April 18, 1848.   7. Nov. 16, 1868.
2. Christmas Eve, 1856.   8. Oct. 7, 1869.
3. Jan. 17, 1865.   9. March 26, 1870.
4. Nov. 6, 1865.   10. April 25, 1870.
5. Jan. 18, 1866.   11. May 17, 1870.
6. Oct. 19, 1867.   12. June 8, 1870.

KNIGHT, Mr. Charles :—
1. June 4, 1844.   6. Aug. 1, 1852.
2. April 13, 1846.   7. Jan. 30, 1854.
3. Feb. 8, 1850.   8. March 17, 1854.
4. July 27, 1851.   9. March 4, 1863.
5. June 29, 1852.   10. March 1, 1864.

* Portions of these letters had already been published by Mr.
Blanchard Jerrold in his Life of his father and elsewhere.

KNOWLES, Mr. Sheridan :—
January 3, 1850.

LANDOR, Walter Savage :—
1. Nov. 22, 1846.
2. Dec. 4, 1850.
3. Sept. 8, 1853.
4. Jan. 7, 1854.
5. July 5, 1856.

LANDSEER, Mr. (afterwards Sir Edwin) :—
May 27, 1844.

LAYARD, Austen H. :—
1. April 3, 1855.
2. April 10, 1855.

LEHMANN, Mrs. :—
1. March 10, 1863.
2. June 29, 1865.
3. Dec. 6, 1868.
4. Feb. 3, 1869.

LEMON, Mr. Mark :—
1. May 3, 1848.
2. Nov. 28, 1848.
3. June 25, 1849.
4. Jan. 31, 1851.
5. Aug. 5, 1852.
6. April 26, 1855.
7. May 23, 1855.
8. Jan. 7, 1856.
9. June 15, 1856.
10. July 2, 1856.

LONGMAN, Mr. Thomas :—
1. 1842 (undated).
2. Nov. 28, 1859.

LONGMAN, Mr. William :—
1839 (undated).

LOVEJOY, Mr. G. :—
(In answer to a requisition of the people of Reading that he
would represent them in Parliament).
1. May 31, 1841.
2. June 10, 1841.

LYTTON, Sir E. Bulwer (afterwards Lord Lytton):—
June 5, 1860.

MACLISE, Daniel :—

1. June 2, 1840.

2. July 22, 1844.

MACREADY, W. C. :—

1. 1837 (undated).
2. 1838 (undated).
3. Dec. 13, 1838.
4. 1839 (undated).
5. July 26, 1839.
6. Sept. 21, 1839.
7. Oct. 25, 1839.
8. Nov. 14, 1839.
9. Aug. 24, 1841.
10. Dec. 28, 1841.
11. March 22, 1842.
12. Nov. 12, 1842.
13. 1842 (undated).
14. January 3, 1844.
15. Oct. 14, 1844.
16. Nov. 28, 1844.
17. Aug. 17, 1845.
18. Sept. 18, 1845.
19. Oct. 17, 1845.
20. Oct. 24, 1846.
21. Nov. 23, 1847.
22. March 2, 1848.
23. May 10, 1848.
24. Aug. 26, 1848.
25. Feb. 27, 1851.
26. May 24, 1851.
27. January 31, 1852.
28. Oct. 5, 1852.

29. Jan. 14, 1853.
30. Aug. 24, 1853.
31. Nov. 1, 1854.
32. June 30, 1855.
33. Oct. 4, 1855.
34. March 22, 1856.
35. March 27, 1856.
36. July 8, 1856.
37. Aug. 8, 1856.
38. Dec. 13, 1856.
39. Jan. 28, 1857.
40. July 13, 1857.
41. Aug. 3, 1857.
42. March 15, 1858.
43. Jan. 2, 1860.
44. June 11, 1861.
45. Oct. 13, 1861.
46. Feb. 19, 1863.
47. March 31, 1863.
48. March 1, 1865.
49. April 22, 1865.
50. June 12, 1865.
51. Dec. 28, 1866.
52. March 21, 1868.
53. June 10, 1868.
54. July 20, 1869.
55. Oct. 18, 1369.
56. March 2, 1870.

MAKEHAM, Mr. John M. :—

June 8, 1870.

MARSTON, Dr. Westland :—
Feb. 3, 1858.

MILNES, Mr. Monckton (afterwards Lord Houghton) :
March 10, 1841.

MITTON, Mr. Thomas :—
1. 1838 (undated).
2. March 6, 1839.
3. January 3, 1842.
4. Jan. 31, 1842.
5. March 22, 1842.
6. Nov. 5, 1844.
7. Feb. 17, 1845.
8. Dec. 3, 1856.
9. June 13, 1865.

OLLIER, Mr. Edmund :—
1. March, 1864.
2. Aug. 3, 1869.

OUVRY, Mr. Frederic :—
1. July 29, 1863.
2. Aug. 22, 1869.

OWEN, Professor :—
July 12, 1865.

PANIZZI, Sir Antonio :—
1. March 14, 1859.
2. March 15, 1859.
3. April 7, 1859.

PARDOE, Miss :—
July 19, 1842.

PARKINSON, J. C. :—
Dec. 25, 1868.

POLLOCK, Sir Frederick :—
March 15, 1864.

POLLOCK, Mrs. Frederick :—
May 2, 1870.

F

POOLE, Mr. John :—
Christmas-Eve, 1850.

POWER, Miss Marguerite :—
1. July 2, 1847.
2. July 14, 1847.
3. Dec. 15, 1856.
4. Sept. 25, 1860.
5. Feb. 26, 1863.

POWER, Mrs. :—
Oct. 23, 1867.

PROCTER, Adelaide Anne :—
Dec. 17, 1854.

PROCTER, B. W. (" Barry Cornwall") :—
1. April 15, 1854.
2. Jan. 2, 1857.
3. Dec. 18, 1858.
4. March 19, 1859.
5. Dec. 31, 1864.
6. Aug. 13, 1866.

PROCTER, Mrs. :—
1. Feb. 15, 1865.
2. Sept. 26, 1865.

READE, Charles :—
Sept. 30, 1863.

REGNIER, Monsieur :—
1. May 9, 1853.
2. May 20, 1853.
3. Feb. 3, 1855.
4. Nov. 21, 1855.
5. Feb. 11, 1858.
6. Feb. 20, 1858.
7. Oct. 15, 1859.
8. Nov. 16, 1859.
9. Feb. 1, 1863.

ROBERTS, David, R.A. :—
1. Jan. 3, 1850.
2. Feb. 21, 1851.
3. March 20, 1851.
4. Feb. 28, 1855.

RUSSELL, Lord John (afterwards Earl Russell) :—
1. June 30, 1852.
2. Sept. 21, 1853.
3. June 17, 1860.
4. Aug. 16, 1865.
5. May 26, 1869.

RYLAND, Mr. Arthur :—
1. Jan. 18, 1854.
2. Jan. 29, 1855.
3. Feb. 26, 1855.
4. Oct. 3, 1857.
5. June 21, 1865.
6. Aug. 13, 1869.
7. Sept. 6, 1869.

SANDYS, Mr. William :—
June 13, 1847.

SAUNDERS, Mr. John :—
Oct. 26, 1854.

SCULTHORPE, Mr. W. R. :—
Nov. 10, 1859.

SMITH, Mr. Arthur :—
1. Jan. 26, 1859.
2. Sept. 3, 1861.

SMITH, Mr. H. P. :—
1. July 14, 1842.
2. June 14, 1847.
3. July 9, 1847.

STANFIELD, Mr. Clarkson :—
1. July 26, 1843.
2. April 30, 1844.
3. Aug. 24, 1844.
4. Oct. 2, 1845.
5. March 6, 1846.
6. May 25, 1849.
7. Jan. 2, 1853.
8. Nov. 3, 1854.
9. May 20, 1855.
10. May 22, 1855.
11. June 20, 1855.
12. Dec. 5, 1862.
13. Sept. 21, 1864.
14. April 18, 1867.

STANFIELD, Mr. George :—
May 19, 1867.

STONE, Mr. Frank :—
1. Nov. 21, 1848.
2. Nov. 23, 1848.
3. Nov. 27, 1848.
4. June 4, 1849.
5. July 20, 1851.
6. Aug. 23, 1851.
7. Dec. 20, 1852.
8. June 23, 1853.

9. May 30, 1854.
10. Oct. 13, 1854.
11.) May 24, 1855. (Two let-
12.) ters of the same date.)
13. June 1, 1857.
14. Aug. 9, 1857.
15. Aug. 17, 1857.
16. Aug. 18, 1857.
17. Dec. 13, 1857.
18. Dec. 13, 1858.
19. Oct. 19, 1859.

STONE, Mr. Marcus :—
1. Dec. 19, 1853.
2. Feb. 23, 1864.
3. Sept. 13, 1865.

STORRAR, Mrs. :—
May 15, 1864.

" SUN," Editor of the :—
April 14, 1848.

TAGART, Rev. Edward :—
1. Aug. 8, 1844.
2. Jan 28, 1847.

TALFOURD, Miss Mary (afterwards Mrs. Major) : —
1. Dec. 16, 1841.
2. March 12, 1863.

TALFOURD, Serjeant : —
July 15, 1838.

TENNENT, Sir Emerson :—
1. Nov. 14, 1853.
2. Jan. 9, 1857.
3. Aug. 26, 1864.
4. Aug. 20, 1866.

THACKERAY (W. M.) :—
Feb. 2, 1858.

THORNBURY, Mr. Walter :—
1. April 18, 1862.
2. Sept. 15, 1866.
3. April 1, 1867.

TOMLIN, Mr. John :—
Feb. 23, 1841.*

* First published in an American (qy. *Graham's ?*) Magazine edited by Edgar Allan Poe, in 1842.

TOOLE, Mr. J. L. :—
Nov. 2, 1867.

TROLLOPE, Mrs. : —
1. Dec. 16, 1842.   2. June 19, 1855.

VIARDOT, Madame :—
Dec. 3, 1855.

WARD, E. M., R.A. :—
March 9, 1861.

WARD, Mrs. E. M. :—
May 11, 1870.

WATKINS, Mr. John :—
1, Oct. 18, 1852.   2. Sept. 28, 1861.

WATSON, Hon. Richard :—
Nov. 27, 1846.

WATSON, Hon. Mrs. :—

1. Jan. 25, 1847.	15. Nov. 22, 1852.
2. July 27, 1848.	16. Aug. 27, 1853.
3. Nov. 30, 1849.	17. Sept. 21, 1853.
4. Sept. 24, 1850.	18. Jan. 13, 1854.
5. Nov. 23, 1850.	19. Nov. 1, 1854.
6. Dec. 9, 1850.	20. Sept. 16, 1855.
7. Dec. 14, 1850.	21. Dec. 23, 1855.
8. Dec. 19, 1850.	22. Oct. 7, 1856.
9. Dec. 30, 1850.	23. May 31, 1859.
10. Jan. 24, 1851.	24. Sept. 14, 1860.
11. Jan. 28, 1851.	25. July 8, 1861.
12. July 11, 1851.	26. Nov. 5, 1867.
13. April 6, 1852.	27. May 11, 1868.
14. Aug. 5, 1852.	

WHITE, Rev. James :—

1. Feb. 24, 1846.
2. May 4, 1848.
3. Sept. 23, 1849.
4. Feb. 5, 1850.
5. July 13, 1850.
6. Oct. 19, 1852.
7. Nov. 22, 1852.
8. Dec. 9, 1852.
9. March 7, 1854.
10. Feb. 8, 1857.
11. May 22, 1857.
12. Nov. 5, 1858.
13. July 7, 1859.

WHITE, Miss Lotty :—

April 18, 1859.

WHITE, Mrs. :—

June 5, 1859.

WILLS, Mr. W. H. :—

1. Feb. 18, 1846.
2. March 2, 1846.
3. March 4, 1846.
4. March 12, 1850.
5. July 27, 1850.
6. Aug. 9, 1850.
7. Feb. 10, 1851.
8. April 3, 1851.
9. Oct. 12, 1852.
10. Oct. 13, 1852.
11. Dec. 9, 1852.
12. Christmas-Eve, 1852.
13. 1853 [undated].*
14. June 13, 1853.
15. June 18, 1853.
16. July 27, 1853.
17. Sept. 18, 1853.
18. Nov. 17, 1853.
19. Nov. 21, 1853.
20. April 12, 1854.
21. June 22, 1854.
22. Feb. 9, 1855.
23. Feb. 16, 1855.
24. Sept. 16, 1855.
25. Oct. 19, 1855.
26. Oct. 21, 1855.
27. Oct. 24, 1855.
28. Jan. 6, 1856.
29. April 6, 1856.
30. Aug. 7, 1856.
31. Sept. 28, 1856.
32. Sept. 4, 1860.
33. Dec. 13, 1861.
34. Dec. 15, 1861.
35. Jan. 2, 1862.
36. Dec. 20, 1863.
37. June 6, 1867.
38. June 13, 1867.
39. Sept. 2, 1867.
40. Nov. 3, 1867.
41. July 31, 1868.
42. June 24, 1869.
43. Jan. 23, 1870.

* Misplaced, probably: refers, apparently, to the projected Christmas Number of *Household Words* for Christmas 1852.

WILSON, Mr. Effingham :—
Nov. 7, 1848.

YATES, Mr. Edmund :—

1. July 19, 1857.	5. March 29, 1859.
2. Nov. 16, 1857.	6. Sept. 23, 1860.
3. Feb. 2, 1858.	7. Oct. 6, 1861.
4. April 28, 1858.	8. Sept. 30, 1865.

YATES, Mrs. (mother of Mr. Edmund Yates) :—
May 15, 1858.

101

LETTERS OF CHARLES DICKENS, *not included in the above collection, addressed to the following correspondents :—*

ANONYMOUS (London Correspondent of a local paper*) :—

Letter dated "48, Doughty-street, Feb. 16, 1838," and signed " Charles Dickens."—Printed in Mackenzie's *Life of Dickens*, pp. 213-214.

ANONYMOUS :—

Letter dated " Devonshire Terrace, Second January, 1844," and signed " Charles Dickens." —Facsimiled in *The Autographic Mirror.* London, February 20, 1864. No. 1, p.7.

* A letter from Dickens, dated "Darlington, Saturday morning" (January, 1838), appeared in the local paper in question.

BAYLIS, Thomas :—

Letter to Thomas Baylis, Esq., dated " Gad's
Hill-place, Dec. 19, 1861," and signed "Charles
Dickens."

BRIT. MUS.—Egerton MSS., 2264, ff. 22, 23.

BENNETT (Sir John) :—

Letter dated " Gad's-hill-place, Sept. 14, 1863,"
and signed "Charles Dickens."—Printed in the
Daily News, Saturday, January 10, 1880.

BENNETT, W. C. :—

Letter dated "Broadstairs, Kent, Aug. 29, 1848,"
and signed " Charles Dickens."—*Testimonials of
Intellectual Ability, Letters from distinguished Men
of the Time to W. C. Bennett* [Privately printed,
1871], pp. 21-22.

BLANCHARD, Laman :—

Two Letters to Laman Blanchard, dated,

    1. " 48, Doughty Street : Sunday morning."
    2. " Elm Cottage, Petersham : Thursday
       night, July 13, 1839,"

and signed "Charles Dickens."—Printed in the
Memoir of Laman Blanchard by Blanchard
Jerrold prefixed to his Poetical Works. Lon-
don : Chatto and Windus, 1876, pp. 37-40.

BLESSINGTON, Lady :—

Eight Letters from Charles Dickens to the Countess of Blessington, dated—

1. Devonshire Terrace, June 2, 1841.
2.   ,,   ,,   March 10, 1844.
3. Covent Garden, 1844 (undated).
4. Milan, Nov. 20, 1844.
5. Genoa, May 9, 1845.
6. Devonshire Terrace, March 2, 1846.
7.   ,,   ,,   May 19, 1846.
8. Paris, Jan. 24, 1847.

Printed in *The Literary Life and Correspondence of the Countess of Blessington, by R. R. Madden.* London: Newby, 1855, vol. iii., pp. 98-107.

BUCKSTONE, J. B. :—

Letter dated "May 15, 1870," and signed " Charles Dickens."—Printed in Mackenzie's *Life of Dickens*, p. 312.

CHORLEY, Henry Fothergill :—

Six letters, signed "Charles Dickens," and dated as follows :—

1. Tavistock House, Feb. 3, 1860.
2. Hyde Park-gate, March 1, 1862.
3. Gad's Hill, Dec. 18, 1863.
4. Office of A. Y. R., Oct. 28, 1865.
5. Gad's Hill, June 2, 1867.
6.   ,,   July 3, 1867.

Printed in the second volume of *Autobiography,*

Memoir, and Letters of Henry Fothergill Chorley.
London: Bentley, 1873, pp. 161-166, pp. 229-236.

CLARKE, Charles and Mary Cowden :—

Charles Dickens and his Letters.—Printed in
*Recollections of Writers, by Charles and Mary
Cowden Clarke.* London : Sampson Low and
Co., 1878, pp. 295-341. .

The letters, addressed to Mary and Charles Cowden Clarke,
are twenty-two in number, and are dated as follows :—

1. Devonshire Terrace, April 14, 1848.
2. „   „   April 16, 1848.
3. „   „   July 1, 1848.
4. „   „   July 22, 1848.
5. Broadstairs, August 5, 1848.
6. „   Sept. 19, 1848 (in facsimile).
7. Devonshire Terrace, January 13, 1849.
8. „   „   May 5, 1849.
9. Great Malvern, March 29, 1851.
10. Devonshire House, May 7, 1851.
11. Tavistock House, March 3, 1852.
12. „   „   December 28, 1852.
13. „   „   November 14, 1853
14. „   „   December 19, 1855.
15. „   „   October 10, 1856.
16. Gad's Hill Place, August 21, 1859.
17. London, April 23, 1860.
18. Friday, January 25, 1861.
19. Gad's Hill Place, July 7, 1862.
20. London, November 3, 1866.
21. „   June 17, 1867.
22. Gad's Hill, November 2, 1867.

CROPPER, Margaret (Lord Denman's fourth daughter):
Letter dated "Tavistock House, January 21,
1853," and signed "Charles Dickens."—
Printed in Sir Joseph Arnould's *Memoir of
Thomas, first Lord Denman.* London : Long-
mans, 1873, vol. ii., pp. 333-334.

FRASER, Thomas :—
Letter to Thomas Fraser, Esq., Morning Chronicle
Office, signed "Charles Dickens," and dated
"George and Pelican, Newbury, Sunday morn-
ing, Nov. 1835."—Printed in *Yesterdays with
Authors,* by James T. Fields. London :
Sampson Low and Co., 1872, p. 232.

FELTON, Mr. C. C. :—
Nine Letters to Mr. C. C. Felton. Printed in
Yesterdays with Authors, by James T. Fields,
pp. 130-154.

The letters are dated as follows:—
1. Washington : March 14, 1842.
2. Niagara Falls : April 29, 1842.
3. Montreal : May 21, 1842.
4. Devonshire Terrace : July 31, 1842.
5.   ,,   ,,   Sept. 1, 1842.
6.   ,,   ,,   Dec. 31, 1842.
7.   ,,   ,,   March 2, 1843.
8. Broadstairs : Sept. 1, 1843.
9. Devonshire Terrace : January 2, 1844.

Fields, James T. : —

Letters to James T. Fields.—Printed in Fields's
Yesterdays with Authors, pp. 154-246.

The letters, thirty-three in number, are dated as follows :—

1. Gad's Hill [June or July, 1859].
2.　　,,　　[July, 1859].
3.　　,,　　July 20, 1859.
4. August 6, 1859.　　　10. July 12, 1867.
5. October, 1862.　　　11. July 25, 1867.
6. May 2, 1866.　　——12. Sept. 3, 1867.
7. October 16, 1866.　　13. October 3, 1867.
8. June 3, 1867.　　-　14. October, 1867.
9. June 13, 1867.　　　15. November, 1867.
16. New York : January 15, 1868.
17. Baltimore : February 9, 1868.
18. Boston : February, 1868.
19. Sunday, March 8, 1868.
20. Albany : March 19, 1868.
21. Sunday, April 26, 1868, and Thursday, April 30.
22. May, 1868.
23. Gad's Hill : May 25, 1868.
24.　　,,　　July 7, 1868.
25. Liverpool : October 30, 1868.
26. Glasgow : December 16, 1868.
27. London : February 15, 1869.
28. Liverpool : April 9, 1869.
29. London : May 5, 1869.
30.　,,　May 19, 1869.
31.　,,　May 25, 1869.
32.　.,　January 14, 1870.
33.　,,　April 18, 1870.

Guy, Mr. :—

Letter dated " Barnum's Hotel (Baltimore),

March 23, 1842," and signed " Charles Dickens." — Printed in Mackenzie's *Life of Dickens*, pp. 144-145.

HARNESS, Rev. William : —

Letter to the Rev. William Harness (undated), signed " Charles Dickens." —Printed in *The Literary Life of the Rev. William Harness, by the Rev. A. G. L'Estrange*. London : Hurst and Blackett, 1871, p. 168.

Invitation to himself and to Miss Harness to " dine with us at the Star and Garter at Richmond, on Monday, the 26th." This note is not printed in the Collected Letters, though three others to the same correspondent are.

HOGARTH, Mr. George :—

Letter to Mr. George Hogarth, dated " 13, Furnival's Inn, January 20, 1835," and signed " Charles Dickens."—Printed in *Forty Years' Recollections of Life, Literature, and Public Affairs, by Charles Mackay*. London : Chapman and Hall, 1877, vol. i. pp. 79-80.

HOOD, Thomas :—

Extracts from a letter of Charles Dickens to Thomas Hood (dated " Devonshire Terrace, Nov. 11, 1842 ?"), printed in a letter from Hood to Dr. Elliot. — *Memorials of Thomas Hood*, Moxon, 1860, vol ii., p. 144.

IRVING, Washington :—

Three Letters from Charles Dickens to Washington Irving, dated "1841," "Washington, March 21, 1842," and "Tavistock House, London, July 5, 1856."—Printed in *The Life and Letters of Washington Irving*, edited by his nephew, Pierre M. Irving. London : Bentley, 1863-4, vol. iii., pp. 128-130 ; 148 ; vol. iv., pp. 195-196.

JAY, John :—

Letter to Mr. John Jay, dated "Devonshire Terrace, London, Sept. 1, 1842," and signed "Charles Dickens."—Printed in the *New York Independent*, December 25, 1879.

JERDAN, William :—

Letter to William Jerdan, dated "Doughty-street, Friday morning," and signed "Charles Dickens."—Printed in *The Autobiography of William Jerdan*. Vol. iv. (1853), pp. 365-366.

Accepting an invitation to an entertainment given to its friends, on the "Literary Gazette" attaining its majority (twenty-five years).

JERROLD, Blanchard :—

Charles Dickens and Douglas Jerrold.—A narrative sent to Mr. Blanchard Jerrold by Charles
Dickens, dated "Tavistock House, Nov. 26,
1858."—Partly printed in the *Life and Remains
of Douglas Jerrold, by his son, Blanchard Jerrold*
(London, 1859), pp. 334-338; and more fully
in *The Best of all Good Company.* § *A Day with
Charles Dickens* (with page of facsimile), pp. 33-
35.

JERROLD, Douglas :—

Three Letters, signed "Charles Dickens," and
dated as follows :—

1. Paris : Feb. 14, 1847.

2. Devonshire Terrace : Nov. 17, 1849.

3. Household Words Office : Feb. 6, 1856.

Printed in *The Best of all Good Company.* § *A Day
with Charles Dickens, edited by Blanchard Jerrold,*
pp. 35-39.

JOLLY, Miss :—

Three Letters to the Authoress of "A Wife's
Story," "An Experience," and other tales
[Miss Jolly], dated "Folkestone, July 17 and

21, 1855," and " Wellington-street, Strand,
July 22, 1869," and signed " Charles Dickens."
Printed as part of a Prefatory Note to *A Wife's
Story and other Tales. By the Author of " Caste."*
London : Hurst and Blackett, 3 vols., 1875.

LEWIS, Hon. Ellis :—

Letter dated " Westminster Hotel, New York,
January 18, 1868," and signed " Charles
Dickens." — Printed in Mackenzie's *Life of
Dickens*, p. 149.

MACKENZIE, R. Shelton :—

Two Letters, dated " Broadstairs, Kent, Aug. 23,
1841," and " Devonshire Terrace, Dec. 10,
1847," and signed " Charles Dickens."—Printed
in Mackenzie's *Life of Dickens*, pp. 174, 218-219.

MACRAE, David :—

Extracts from Letters addressed by Charles
Dickens in 1861 to Mr. David Macrae.—
Printed in *Home and Abroad : Sketches and
Gleanings by David Macrae*. Glasgow, 1871,
pp. 127-128.

MARRYAT, Captain Frederick :—

Four Letters to Captain Marryat, signed " Charles

Dickens," and dated "Devonshire Terrace, July 16, 1842," "Devonshire Terrace, January 3," "Broadstairs, Sept. 6, 1843," "Brighton, Monday, March 6, 1848."—Printed in *Life and Letters of Captain Marryat.* London : Richard Bentley & Son, 1872, vol. ii., pp. 118-119 ; 143-145 ; 283-284.

MENKEN, Adah Isaacs :—

Letter dated "Gad's Hill-place, October 21, 1867," and signed "Charles Dickens."—Facsimiled in a volume of Poems, entitled "*Infelicia, by Adah Isaacs Menken*," 1868, which is dedicated to Dickens.

MOORE, George :—

Letter to Mr. George Moore, undated (1859,) signed "Charles Dickens." — Printed in a volume entitled *George Moore, Merchant and Philanthropist*, by Samuel Smiles. London : Routledge, 1878, p. 217.

NAPIER, Macvey :—

Four Letters to Mr. Macvey Napier, dated "Devonshire Terrace, Jan. 21, 1843," "Broadstairs, Sept. 16, 1843," "Devonshire

G

Terrace, July 28, 1845," and " Nov. 10, 1845."
*Selection from the Correspondence of the late
Macvey Napier, Esq.* London : Macmillan,
1879, pp. 416-418 ; 432-433 ; 502-504 ; 505.

O'DRISCOLL, W. J. :—

Letter to W. J. O'Driscoll, dated " Gad's Hill
Place, Wednesday, May 18, 1870," and signed
" Charles Dickens."—Printed in the Preface to
*A Memoir of Daniel Maclise, R.A., by W. Justin
O'Driscoll.* London : Longmans, 1871.

PHILP, Mr. Franklin :—

Letter dated " Baltimore, January 28, 1868," and
signed " Charles Dickens."—Printed in Mackenzie's *Life of Dickens*, p. 279.

RAWLINSON, Mr. Robert :—

Letter dated " Tavistock House, January 25,
1854," and signed " Charles Dickens." —
Printed in *The Times*, Friday, February 6, 1880.

SALA, George Augustus :—

Letter to Mr. G. A. Sala, dated " Tavistock
House, Friday, September 19, 1856," and
signed " Charles Dickens."—Printed in the

Preface to Mr. Sala's Essay on Charles Dickens. London : Routledge and Sons [1870], pp. ix., x.

SEYMOUR, Robert :—

Letter to R. Seymour, dated " April, 1836." Printed at pp. 7-8 of the Life of Robert Seymour, prefixed to a Collection of Seymour's Sketches. London : John Camden Hotten [1867].

SMITH, Arthur :—

Letter dated " Tavistock House, May 25, 1858," with a note giving permission to show it, dated " Tavistock House, May 28, 1858," signed " C. D." — Printed in Mackenzie's *Life of Dickens*, pp. 248-250.

First printed in the *New York Tribune*, and copied afterwards into some of the English journals. " It had been addressed and given to Mr. Arthur Smith, as an authority for correction of false rumours and scandals, and Mr. Smith had given a copy of it, with like intention, to the *Tribune* correspondent in London. Its writer referred to it always afterwards as his ' violated letter.' "—FORSTER'S *Life of Dickens*.

STONE, Mr. Frank :—

Letter dated " Devonshire Terrace, May 24, 1849," and signed " Charles Dickens."— Printed in Mackenzie's *Life of Dickens*, p. 220.

TALFOURD, Mr. Serjeant :—

Three Letters dated "Devonshire-Terrace, April 27" (1840), "Feb. 16, 1841," and "March 22, 1841," and signed "Charles Dickens."— Printed in Mackenzie's *Life of Dickens*, pp. 214-215; 216, 217.

TEGG, Mr. Thomas :—

Letter to Mr. Thomas Tegg, dated "15, Furnivals Inn, Wednesday morning," and signed "Charles Dickens."—Printed in *Notes and Queries*, 5th S., iii., p. 366 (May 8, 1875).

Upon the subject of Mr. Dickens writing a work for Mr. Tegg, entitled *Serjeant Bell and his Raree Show*. The terms were agreed upon and accepted ; but for some reason the scheme fell through, and nothing came of it.

THACKERAY, W. M. :—

Letter to W. M. Thackeray, dated "Tavistock House, Wednesday, November 24, 1858," and signed "Charles Dickens."—Printed in a pamphlet entitled *Mr. Thackeray, Mr. Yates, and the* *Garrick Club, the Correspondence and Facts, stated by Edmund Yates. Printed for private circulation,* 1859, p. 13.

THORNBURY, Walter :—

Letter to Mr. Walter Thornbury, dated "Gad's hill-place, Monday, August 5, 1867," and signed "Charles Dickens."—Printed in *Notes and Queries*, 5th S., vii., p. 326 (April 28, 1877).

Refers to the series of "Old Stories Re-told," which Mr. Thornbury was at that time writing for *All the Year Round*.

YOUNG, Charles Mayne:—

Letter to Charles Mayne Young, dated "Office of Household Words, July 1, 1852," and signed "Charles Dickens."—Printed in *A Memoir of Charles Mayne Young, Tragedian, with Extracts from his Son's Journal*. London : Macmillan, 1871, vol. ii., pp. 158-159.

SPEECHES.

102

The Newsvendors' Benevolent and Provident Institution.—Speeches in behalf of the Institution by the late Mr. Charles Dickens, President. London : printed by Buck and Wootton, 126, Westminster-bridge-road [1871], pp. 15, in coloured wrapper.

Contains Summary of Speeches of 21st November, 1849, and 27th January, 1852 ; also copy of letter to Secretary, dated "Tavistock House, April 13, 1854," and signed "Charles Dickens."

103

Speech of Charles Dickens, Esq., delivered at the meeting of the Administrative Reform Association, at the Theatre Royal, Drury Lane, Wednesday, June 27, 1855. — London : Effingham Wilson, 1855, pp. 11 (including title).

104

Speech of Charles Dickens as Chairman of the Anniversary Festival Dinner of the Royal Free Hospital, held at the Freemasons' Tavern on 6th May, 1863.

With prefatory remarks dated "Royal Free Hospital, Gray's-inn-road, London, June 24, 1870," and signed "James S. Blyth, Secretary." (Privately printed, pp. 8.)

105

THE CHARLES DICKENS DINNER.—An Authentic Record of the Public Banquet given to Mr. Charles Dickens, at the Freemasons' Hall, London, on Saturday, November 2, 1867, prior to his departure for the United States. With a Report of the Speeches from special shorthand notes. London : Chapman and Hall, 1867, pp. 82.

With two pages of introductory matter by Mr. Charles Kent, the Honorary Secretary, dated "Wednesday, November 6, 1867," and signed "C. K."

106

Address delivered at the Birmingham and Midland Institute, 27th September, 1869, by Charles Dickens. Birmingham, royal 8vo, pp. 15, green wrapper.

107

SPEECHES LITERARY AND SOCIAL. BY CHARLES DICKENS. Now first collected. With chapters on Charles Dickens as a Letter-writer, Poet, and Public Reader. London : John Camden Hotten [1870], pp. 372.

The Introduction, which occupies the first forty-seven pages, is dated "December, 1869 ; " but the volume, although the greater part of it was then in type, was not actually published until after

Dickens's death in 1870. It was edited, prefaced, and annotated by the Editor of the present Bibliography, the first rough sketch of which will be found at pp. 358-365.

The fifty-six Speeches comprised in the above volume were delivered at the following places and dates :—

1. Edinburgh : June 25, 1841.
2. United States : Jan., 1842.
3. Boston : Feb. 1, 1842.
4. Hartford : Feb. 7, 1842.
5. New York : Feb. 18, 1842.
6. Manchester : Oct. 5, 1843.
7. Liverpool : Feb. 26, 1844.
8. Birmingham : Feb. 28, 1844.
9. London : April 6, 1846.
10. Leeds : Dec. 1, 1847.
11. Glasgow : Dec. 28, 1847.
12. London : March 1, 1851.
13. London : April 14, 1851.
14. London : May 10, 1851.
15. London : June 9, 1851.
16. London : June 14, 1852.
17. Birmingham : Jan. 6, 1853.
18. London : April 30, 1853.
19. London : May 1, 1853.
20. Birmingham : Dec. 30, 1853.
21. London : Dec. 30, 1854.
22. Drury Lane : June 27, 1855.
23. Sheffield : Dec. 22, 1855.
24. London : March 12, 1856.
25. London : Nov. 5, 1857.
26. London : Feb. 9, 1858.
27. Edinburgh : March 26, 1858.
28. London : March 29, 1858.

29. London : April 29, 1858.
30. London : May 1, 1858.
31. London : May 8, 1858.
32. London : July 21, 1858.
33. Manchester : Dec. 3, 1858.
34. Coventry : Dec. 4, 1858.
35. London : March 29, 1862.
36. London : May 20, 1862.
37. London : May 11, 1864.
38. London : May 9, 1865.
39. London : May 20, 1865.
40. Knebworth : July 29, 1865.
41. London : Feb. 14, 1866.
42. London : March 28, 1866.
43. London : May 7, 1866.
44. London : June 5, 1867.
45. London : Sept. 17, 1867.
46. London : Nov. 2, 1867.
47. Boston : April 8, 1868.
48. New York : April 18, 1868.
49. New York : April 20, 1868.
50. Liverpool : April 10, 1869.
51. Sydenham : Aug. 30, 1869.
52. Birmingham : Sept. 27, 1869.
53. Birmingham : Jan. 6, 1870.
54. St. James's Hall : March 15, 1870.
55. London : April 5, 1870.
56. London : May 2, 1870.

A N A .

———

1

The Reception of Mr. Dickens. With a steel portrait, drawn and engraved by A. Halbert from a
bust by H. Dexter.—*United States Magazine and
Democratic Review*, April, 1842, pp. 315-320.

2

Dickens's American Notes. — *Edinburgh Review*,
January, 1843 (vol. lxxvi., pp. 497-522); reprinted
in *Reviews and Discussions Literary, Political and
Historical*, by James Spedding. London : C.
Kegan Paul & Co., 1879, pp. 240-276 (with long
added Note by the writer).

3

CHARLES DICKENS, with portrait after a drawing by
Miss M. Gillies.—*A New Spirit of the Age*, edited
by R. H. Horne. London : Smith, Elder, & Co.,
1844, vol. i., pp. 1-76.

4

Boz versus Dickens.—*Parker's London Magazine*,
No. II.. February, 1845, pp. 122-128. (London :
John W. Parker, West Strand.)

5

The Fictions of Dickens upon Solitary Confinement.
—*Prisons and Prisoners*, by Joseph Adshead. London : Longman & Co., 1845, pp. 95-121.

6

The People's Portrait Gallery § Charles Dickens. The letter-press by William Howitt, with portrait engraved by W. J. Linton from a picture by Margaret Gillies.—*The People's Journal*, edited by John Saunders. London : 1846, vol. i., pp. 8-12.

7

Notice of the final (double) number (Part xix.-xx.) of *Dombey and Son*.—Printed in *The Sun*, London, Thursday Evening, April 13, 1848.

By Mr. Charles Kent. Dickens was so much pleased with this notice that he wrote a warm letter of thanks, which he desired the Editor to convey to the then unknown anonymous writer. This led to a life-long friendship between the novelist and his reviewer. (See *Letters of Charles Dickens*, vol. i., pp. 186-188). Mr. Kent became proprietor of *The Sun* newspaper early in 1865.

8

The Living Authors of England, by Thomas Powell : New York, 1849 ; Pictures of the Living Authors of Britain, by Thomas Powell. London : Partridge and Oakey, 1851.

The chapter on Charles Dickens occupies pp. 153-178 of the American, and pp. 88-115 of the English edition.

9

Notice of Barnaby Rudge. By Edgar Allan Poe.— *The Literati, some honest opinions about autorial merits and demerits,* &c. *By Edgar A. Poe.* New York, 1850, pp. 464-482.

10

Charles Dickens. Eine Charakteristik von Dr. Julian Schmidt. Leipzig : Verlag von Carl B. Lorck, 1852, pp. 74.

11

Uncle Tom's Cabin, Bleak House, Slavery and Slave Trade. Six articles by Lord Denman, reprinted from the *Standard.*—London : Longmans, 1853, pp. 51.

12

Dickens's Bleak House.—*Spectator,* Sept. 24, 1853 ; reprinted in *Essays by the late George Brimley.* Cambridge : Macmillan & Co., 1858, pp. 289-301.

13

Immortelles from Charles Dickens. By Ich. London: John Moxon, 28, Maddox-street, Regent-street. 1856, pp. 195.

14

The License of Modern Novelists.—*Edinburgh Review*, July, 1857 (vol. cvi., pp. 124-156).

A notice of *Little Dorrit* (in connexion with Charles Reade's *Never too late to Mend* and Mrs. Gaskell's *Life of Charlotte Brontë*) which elicited a retort from the author (see "Curious Misprint in the Edinburgh Review," *suprà*, § 67, p. 33).

15

Royal Literary Fund.—A Summary of Facts drawn from the records of the Society, and issued by the Committee in answer to allegations contained in a pamphlet entitled "The Case of the Reformers of the Literary Fund : stated by Charles W. Dilke, Charles Dickens, and John Forster," together with a Report of the Proceedings at the last Annual Meeting, March 12, 1858 (privately printed), pp. 34.

16

Charles Dickens (1858).—*Literary Studies by the late Walter Bagehot.* London : Longmans, 1879, vol. ii., pp. 184-220.

17

Novels and Novelists from Elizabeth to Victoria. By J. Cordy Jeaffreson. London : Hurst and Blackett, 1858.

The notice of Charles Dickens occupies Chapter xv. (pp. 303-334) of the second volume, the frontispiece to which is a portrait of Dickens, engraved by J. H. Baker.

18

British Novelists and their Styles : being a Critical Sketch of the History of British Prose Fiction. By David Masson, M.A. Cambridge : Macmillan and Co., 1859.

Pages 233-253 are devoted to a consideration of Dickens and Thackeray.

19

Dickens's Dogs ; or the Landseer of Fiction.— *London Society, an Illustrated Magazine,* July, 1863 (vol. iv., pp. 48-61).

20

Two English Essayists : Charles Lamb and Charles Dickens. By Percy Fitzgerald. Printed in *The Afternoon Lectures on Literature and Art,* Second Series. London : Bell and Daldy. 1864.

The portion of the lecture devoted to Dickens occupies pp. 85-100.

21

Histoire de la Littérature Anglaise. *Par H. Taine.*
Tom. iv. *Les Contemporains.* Paris, 1864.

Livre v., chapitre 1. *Le Roman : Dickens*, pp. 3-69.

History of English Literature. *By H. A. Taine,*
translated from the French by H. Van Laun. Edinburgh : Edmonston and Douglas, 1874.

Vol. iv., chapter 1. " *The Novel—Dickens*," pp. 115-162.

22

The Genius of Dickens. By E. P. Whipple.—
Atlantic Monthly, May, 1867 (vol. xix., pp. 546-
554).

23

The Dickens Controversy.—Printed in the *American
Publishers' Circular* of June 1, 1867, with letter
to Messrs. Ticknor and Fields, dated " Gad's Hill-
place, April 16, 1867," and signed " Charles
Dickens."

Reprinted in the form of an Addendum of six pages at the
end of Dr. Shelton Mackenzie's Life of Dickens.

24

CHARLES DICKENS'S USE OF THE BIBLE.—Temple
Bar, September, 1869 (vol. xxvii., pp. 225-234).

25

Charles Dickens. By George Augustus Sala. Lon.

don: George Routledge and Sons [1870], pp. x.

144.

The first sketch of this essay on the genius and character of
Charles Dickens appeared on the day following his death in the
Daily Telegraph (June, 10, 1870). It is here amplified to four
times its original length.

26

In Memoriam. (A memorial notice of Charles

Dickens, by Sir Arthur Helps.)—*Macmillan's Maga-

zine*, July, 1870 (vol. xxii., pp. 236-240).

27

Charles Dickens. By Alfred Austin.—*Temple Bar*,

July, 1870 (vol. xxix., pp. 554-562).

28

Sermon preached by Arthur Penrhyn Stanley, Dean

of Westminster, in Westminster Abbey, June 19,

1870, being the Sunday following the funeral of

Charles Dickens. London: Macmillan and Co.,

1870, pp. 16.

29

Parables of Fiction : A Memorial Discourse on

Charles Dickens. By James Panton Ham. [De-

livered in Essex-street Chapel, Strand, on Sunday,

July 3, 1870.]   Published by Request.   London:
Trübner and Co., 1870, pp. 16.

30

CHARLES DICKENS.   THE STORY OF HIS LIFE.   By
the Author of the Life of Thackeray.   With Illustrations and Facsimiles.   London : John Camden
Hotten [1870], pp. 367.

Compiled by the publisher from materials mainly supplied by
Mr. H. T. Taverner.   The Preface is dated " London, June 29,
1870."

31

THE CHARLES DICKENS SALE.—Catalogue (printed
in facsimile) of the Beautiful Collection of Modern
Pictures, Water Colour Drawings, and Objects of
Art of the late Charles Dickens, with the whole
of the names of purchasers and enormous prices
realised appended to each lot.   Sold by auction
by Messrs. Christie, Manson, and Woods, at their
Great Rooms, 8, King-street, St. James's-square,
on Saturday, July 9, 1870. 4to.   Field and Tuer,
50, Leadenhall-street, pp. 11, in wrapper.

32

Some Memories of Charles Dickens.   By J. T. Fields.
Atlantic Monthly, August, 1870 (vol. xxvi., pp.
235-245).

33

LIFE OF CHARLES DICKENS. By R. SHELTON
MACKENZIE, LL.D., with Personal Recollections
and Anecdotes, Letters by " Boz " never before
published, and uncollected Papers in prose and
verse, pp. 484. Philadelphia : J. B. Peterson and
Brothers.

34

Four Months with Charles Dickens, during his first
visit to America (in 1842). By his Secretary
[G. W. Putnam]. — Printed in *The Atlantic
Monthly*, October and November, 1870 (vol. xxvi.,
pp. 476-482, 591-599).

35

Charles Dickens. A Lecture by Professor Ward,
delivered in the Hulme Town Hall, Manchester,
November 30, 1870 *(Science Lectures, Second
Series*, No. 5, pp. 236-259). Manchester : John
Heywood.

36

MODERN MEN OF LETTERS HONESTLY CRITICISED.
By J. Hain Friswell. London : Hodder and
Stoughton, 1870.

The chapter on Charles Dickens occupies the first forty-five
pages of the book.

H

37

A CHRISTMAS MEMORIAL OF CHARLES DICKENS, by A.
B. Hume. 1870.

This memorial contains a facsimile of Charles Dickens's
Letter to Mr. J. M. Makeham, dated "June 8, 1870," and an
Ode to his memory, "written," says Mr. Forster, "with feeling
and spirit."

38

MR. DICKENS'S AMATEUR THEATRICALS. A Reminis-
cence.—*Macmillan's Magazine*, January, 1871 (vol.
xxiii., pp. 206-215).

39

Bygone Celebrities. By R. H. Horne, Author of
Orion.

1. The Guild of Literature and Art at Chats-
worth.

2. Mr. Nightingale's Diary.

—Printed in the *Gentleman's Magazine*, vol. vi.,
N. S., pp. 247-262 ; 660-672 (February and May,
1871).

40

The Best of all Good Company : a Series of Daily
Companions &c., edited by Blanchard Jerrold.
Part 1.—A Day with Charles Dickens (large 8vo
in yellow wrapper, pp. 62).

The Introductory leaf is dated "June, 1871." Prefixed to the *brochure* is a folding-leaf of facsimile of a portion of a manuscript letter addressed to Mr. Blanchard Jerrold by Charles Dickens and containing recollections of his father, Douglas Jerrold.

41

Dickens at Gadshill.—Lines, signed C. K. [Charles Kent], printed in *The Athenæum* of June 3, 1871 (p. 687).

42

DIALOGUES FROM DICKENS. First and Second Series. 2 vols. fcp. 8vo, pp. 260, 335. Arranged by W. Eliot Fette, A.M.—Boston : Lee and Shepard, 1870-1871.

43

PEN PHOTOGRAPHS OF CHARLES DICKENS'S READINGS. Taken from Life by Kate Field. [1868.] Boston: Loring, pp. 58 (double columns).

New and Enlarged Edition, with portrait and illustrations, pp. iv. 152. (Preface dated December 25, 1870.) Boston : James R. Osgood and Co., 1871.

44

CHARLES DICKENS AS A READER. By Charles Kent. London : Chapman and Hall, 1872, pp. vii. 271, with two facsimiles of pages in the Reading-books.

45

Mr. Dickens and his Critics,
Mr. Dickens as a Reader,

—*Miscellanies—Stories and Essays*—by John Hol-lingshead. London: Tinsley Brothers, 1874, pp. 270-283.

46

THE YOUTH OF DICKENS.—*Chambers's Journal*, January 13 and 20, 1872, pp. 17-21, 40-45.

THE MIDDLE AGE OF DICKENS.—*Chambers's Journal*, February 1, 1873, pp. 74-79.

By James Payn, Author of *The Foster-Brothers*.

47

Dickens in relation to Criticism. By George Henry Lewes.—*Fortnightly Review*, February, 1872, vol. xi., N. S., pp. 141-154.

48

THE DICKENS DICTIONARY: A Key to the Characters and Principal Incidents in the Tales of Charles Dickens. By Gilbert A. Pierce, with additions by William A. Wheeler. Illustrated. Boston: James R. Osgood and Co., 1872, pp. xv. 573. London: Chapman and Hall, 1878 (with Preface by Charles Dickens, jun., pp. xvi. 607).

49

A CYCLOPÆDIA OF THE BEST THOUGHTS OF CHARLES
DICKENS. Compiled and alphabetically arranged
by F. G. de Fontaine. New York : E. J. Hale·
and Son, Murray-street, 1873, pp. 564 (printed
in double columns).

50

Charles Dickens. By Walter Irving. Edinburgh :
Maclachlan and Stewart. London : Simpkin,
Marshall and Co., pp. 30, 1874.

51

Bric - a - Brac Series.—Anecdote Biographies of
Thackeray and Dickens. Edited by Richard
Henry Stoddard.—New York : Scribner, Arm-
strong and Co., 1874.

The Biography of Dickens occupies pp. 197-299 of the volume.

52

THE LIFE OF CHARLES DICKENS. BY JOHN FORSTER.
[In Three Volumes, with portraits, facsimiles, and
other illustrations.] London: Chapman and Hall,
1872-1874. Vol. I., 1812-1842, pp. xviii. 398,
published 1872 ; Vol. II., 1842-1852, pp. xx. 462,

published 1873 ; Vol. III., 1852-1870, pp. xv. 552, published 1874.

Library Edition. In Two Volumes. London: Chapman and Hall, 1876. Vol. I., 1812-1847. pp. xvi. 528; Vol. II., 1847-1870, pp. xiv. 528.

53

"Our Mutual Friend" in Manuscript.—*Scribner's Monthly, an Illustrated Magazine*, vol. viii., pp. 472-475 (August, 1874).—Scribner and Co., New York.

The MSS. of "Our Mutual Friend" was presented by the author, in January, 1866, to Mr. E. S. Dallas, and passed out of his possession into that of Mr. George W. Childs, of Philadelphia.

54

IN AND OUT OF DOORS WITH CHARLES DICKENS. By James T. Fields. Boston : James R. Osgood and Co., 1876, pp. 170.

Reissued from "Yesterdays with Authors." London, 1872, pp 127-250.

55

DICKENS'S LONDON ; or London in the Works of Charles Dickens, by T. Edgar Pemberton. London: Samuel Tinsley, 1876, pp. 260.

56

Dickens and the Pickwick Papers. By Edwin P. Whipple.—*Atlantic Monthly*, August, 1876 (vol. xxxviii., pp. 219-224).

Oliver Twist. By Edwin P. Whipple.—*Atlantic Monthly*, October, 1876 (vol. xxxviii., pp. 474-479).

57

Darwin, Carlyle, and Dickens, with other Essays, by Samuel Davey. London : James Clarke and Co., *n.d.*

The Essay on Charles Dickens occupies pp. 119-156.

58

Our Letter, by M. F. Armstrong, with facsimile of a Letter dated " Gad's Hill-place, Monday, 10th Feb., 1862," and signed " Charles Dickens."— *St. Nicholas. Scribner's Illustrated Magazine for Girls and Boys.* New York, May, 1877 (vol. iv., pp. 438-441).

The letter itself, with a brief extract from the lengthy narrative preceding it, is reprinted in the Collected Letters, vol. ii., pp. 175-176.

59

Charles Dickens's Manuscripts.—*Chambers's Journal*, November 10, 1877, pp. 710-712.

60

THE MODERN NOVEL—Dickens, Bulwer, Thackeray. *Essays in Biography and Criticism, by Peter Bayne, M.A. First Series.* Boston : Gould and Lincoln, 1857, pp. 363-392.

STUDIES OF ENGLISH AUTHORS. By Peter Bayne,
LL.D. No. V. Charles Dickens.—Printed in
The Literary World, March 21 to May 30, 1879.

61

BIBLIOGRAPHY OF THE WRITINGS OF CHARLES DICKENS,
*with many curious and interesting particulars relating
to his Works. By James Cook.* Paisley : J. & J.
Cook, Printers and Publishers, 1879, pp. 80.
London, F. Kerslake, 1879, with Appendix, pp. 88,
in wrapper.

For the more recondite matters which give the chief if not
the sole value to a compilation of this kind, the reader will search
this bulky *brochure* in vain. Nor is the record of more commonly
known and accessible details anywhere thoroughly reliable either
as to accuracy or completeness. And the sins of commission are
as great and grievous as the sins of omission. Mr. Cook's un-
wieldy pamphlet may be said to resemble a waste ground, with a
notice-board attracting the passer's eyes and bearing the legend,
" Rubbish shot here." What can it avail a bibliographer of
Dickens to know or to tell how this or that piratical dunce or
dullard published an imitation or a continuation of the *Pickwick
Papers*, of *Oliver Twist*, of *Nickleby*, or of *Dombey* (pp. 50-51) ;
how an obscure would-be artist issued a worthless series of catch-
penny "extra illustrations (pp. 17, *sqq.*) now so rare as to fetch ten
times their original price " from the pockets of collectors " more
enviable for superfluity of cash than commendable for sufficiency
of understanding ; " how such and such inept or inane Grub-
street garretteers attempted to solve the *Mystery of Edwin Drood*
without having first solved the mysteries of English orthography
and syntax (p. 51) ; how Mr. So-and-so, the notorious West-end

bookseller, foisted upon an unwary collector a made-up set of original editions, "elegantly bound by Pratt in his best manner," for five times their published price (pp. 48-49) ; or how Mr. This-or-that, his bibliopolic neighbour, administered a judicious and well-merited snubbing to the compiler by declining to answer an impertinent inquiry as to the names and addresses of private customers who had purchased sumptuously illustrated copies of Mr. Forster's Life of the novelist, and other curiosities (pp. 67, 72-73) ; or what were the titles of, and who were the contributors to, the Christmas numbers and "extra summer numbers" of the New Series of *All the Year Round*, under the conduct of Charles Dickens, junior (p. 60).

Mr. Cook's pamphlet is also disfigured by a considerable number of *errata*, which should be corrected in a future edition ; *e.g. inter alia :—*

page 13 (three lines from bottom), for "soubriquet" read "sobriquet."

page 21, line 15, for "Lord Cockburn" read "Lord Jef-frey," and for "Thackeray and Cockburn" in the margin, read "Thackeray and Jeffrey."

page 26, line 6, for "Carlile" read "Carlyle."

page vi. line 5, page 27, lines 6 and 7, page 57 (near the middle), for "A Holiday Romance" read "Holiday Romance."

page 28 (four lines from bottom), for "at the" read "on the."

page 29, line 28, for "Jan. 1, 1846," read "Jan. 21, 1846."

page 30, line 12, for "No. 6" read "No. 2."

page 31, line 9, and page 32, line 12, for "A Fly-leaf in Life" read "A Flyleaf in a Life."

page 33, line 4, for "greater actor" read "great actor."

page 33, line 15 (and p. vi., eleven lines from bottom), for "Proctor" read "Procter."

page 37, line 13, for "began" read "begun."

page 39 (nine lines from bottom), for "19 Piccadilly" read "193 Piccadilly."

page 47, line 17, for "bibliomoniacs" read "bibliomaniacs."

page 52, line 21, for "Little Dorrit" read "Little Dombey."

page 56, line 24, for "Ward, Locke & Tyler," read "Ward, Lock & Tyler."

page 57, line 28, for "Explanations" read "Explanation."

page 62, line 13, for "25th Jan." read "25th June."

page 62, line 26, for "1865" read "1868."

page 62, line 28, for "fac-similies" read "fac-similes."

page 63 (seven lines from bottom), for "Mayal" read "Mayall."

page 65, line 6, for "Dicken's" read "Dickens."

page 67, line 17, for "Wellford" read "Welford."

page 75, line 4, for "January 1848" read "January 1838."

page 80, line 19, for "Lowe" read "Low."

page 81, lines 31 and 34, for "Lee & Shepherd" read "Lee and Shepard."

page 81 (four lines from bottom), for "Idah" read "Adah."

page 83, line 9, for "Savonarolo" read "Savonarola."

page 85 (seven lines from bottom), for "J. Webster" read "T. Webster."

page 86, lines 1 and 5, for "Miss La Crevy" read "Miss La Creevy."

page 88 (four lines from bottom), for "lonlieness" read "loneliness."

62

CHARLES DICKENS AS A JOURNALIST. By Charles Kent. — Printed in *The Journalist, a Monthly Phonographic Magazine* (F. Pitman, 20, Paternoster-row), London, December, 1879 (vol. i. pp. 17-25).

63

Great Novelists : Scott, Thackeray, Dickens, Lytton. By James Crabb Watt, Edinburgh : Macniven and Wallace. 1880.

The chapter on Dickens occupies pp. 163-218.

64

IN KENT WITH CHARLES DICKENS. By Thomas Frost. London : Tinsley Brothers, 1880, pp. viii. 312.

THE END.